THAT LEFT TURN
◀◀◀ AT ◀◀◀
ALBUQUERQUE

THAT LEFT TURN
◀◀◀ AT ◀◀◀
ALBUQUERQUE

SCOTT PHILLIPS

Published in the United States by
Soho Press, Inc.
227 W 17th Street
New York, NY 10011

Library of Congress Cataloging-in-Publication Data

Phillips, Scott, author.
That left turn at albuquerque / Scott Phillips.

ISBN 978-1-64129-109-5
eISBN 978-1-64129-110-1

1. Organized crime—Fiction. 2. Art—Forgeries—Fiction.
3. Suspense fiction.
PS3566.H515 T48 2020 | DDC 813'.54—dc23

Printed in the United States of America

10 9 8 7 6 5 4 3 2 1

THAT LEFT TURN ◀◀◀ AT ◀◀◀ ALBUQUERQUE

CHAPTER ONE

HEADING UP THE 5 and in a hyper-enervated state, he stopped in Mission Viejo at Manny's Liquor and Variety Store, where he knew a working pay phone was attached to the brick wall outside. Scored and pitted, covered with graffiti and rust, for all Rigby knew it might have been the last one in Southern California. Next to it stood a skeletal derelict with a week's growth of beard and stiff, ancient jeans gray with filth, looking as though he was waiting for a call. Rigby decided to go inside and buy a celebratory bottle, in case the tweaker decided to shove off on his own.

This might be the seedier side of Mission Viejo, but that still meant a fine selection of champagnes and a patronizing sales clerk. "We have a nice Veuve Clicquot here for sixty-four ninety-nine," he said, nostrils flaring, eyeing him sidelong. "I imagine that'd do you nicely." Minus the condescension, that would have been fine for Rigby's purposes, but he felt compelled to put the salesman in his place.

"That's white trash booze," he said. "How much for the Krug?"

"That's vintage. 2003."

"Swell. How much?"

"Three hundred nineteen dollars and ninety-nine cents."

"Great, and stick a bow on it."

Outside, the stick figure was still standing by the phone.

Rigby would have preferred not to have to interact with anyone in the context of this particular call, but the man gave no sign that he intended to get lost. Once Rigby had placed the champagne in the car, he walked up to the phone, jingling the quarters in his pocket.

"Phone's in use right now," the tweaker said.

"Doesn't look that way to me."

"Waiting for a call. Urgent."

"That's not the same as in use."

"This is my phone, buddy."

His initial instinct was to ratchet the conflict up, preferably ending with his throwing the tweaker into an arroyo somewhere, but making the least possible impression was important here, so he reached into his wallet and pulled out a ten. "Here. I need privacy for ten minutes."

The tweaker snorted and looked away. "Ten bucks. Jesus, last of the big fuckin' spenders here."

Rigby crumpled the ten in his fist and focused on calming himself. He could easily lift this man over his head, snap his spine in two, could in fact do any number of things that would attract attention and ruin his chance to make an untraceable phone call.

"What you want, then?"

"A hundred."

"Fifty."

"Fuck you. A Benjamin or I ain't moving."

Again he resisted his natural impulse to escalate the situation, instead reaching back into his wallet and extracting a beautiful new hundred-dollar bill. The tweaker took it with a demented, near-toothless grin and scooted away across the parking lot and down the sidewalk before disappearing into a copse of dried-up trees. Just as Rigby was about to pick up the receiver, the phone rang and he picked up.

"Yeah?"

"Jason," said a raspy voice on the other end of the line. "The Brewster."

"Jason's not here."

"The fuck? He was supposed to be waiting."

"Yeah, last time I saw him he was talking to some cops. Looked like narcs to me." He hung up, then picked up again and waited for a dial tone, then started filling the thing with quarters. He punched in the number from memory, having burned the paper he'd written it down on.

"Yo, Crumdog's phone."

"Hi, Crumdog."

"This ain't Crumdog. I answer his phone for him. The fuck is this?"

"This is Lancer. Pooty was supposed to tell Crumdog I was calling."

There was a silence of fifteen or twenty seconds, and then a hoarse voice came on. "Yeah?"

"Pooty tell you I was calling?"

"Don't know anybody named Pooty."

"I did some work for Pooty a while back, got some charges dropped and it didn't cost him a cent. Now he's doing me a favor."

"Might have heard about that."

"He didn't tell you Lancer was going to be in touch?"

"He might have mentioned something."

"Look, I got something I'd like to unload. Pooty thought you might be glad to get it."

"Pooty thinks a lot of things don't necessarily jibe with reality."

"Should I go somewhere else, then?"

"I didn't say that. Fuck. All right, if it's what Pooty Tang says it is, and I'm not saying I believe that, then we could do some business. You send someone and I'll send someone and we'll have them meet halfway. How far you at from Topeka?"

"Topeka? I'm on the West Coast."

"Shit. All right, I don't want a civilian crossing the whole fucking country with product."

"I heartily agree."

"Yeah. My man'll meet yours in Needles, know it?"

"I know it, but why don't we meet, you and me?"

"Jesus fucking Christ, you're making me wonder if you're too fucking green to do business with. You're talking on a burner, right?"

"Pay phone."

"Where'd you find one of those? Fuck it, don't matter. Get yourself a burner next time you wanna talk."

"I'll have my man in Needles tomorrow night."

"What the fuck ever, 'Lancer.' Just know that if you fuck me over I will learn your real name and the Devil's Hammers will make your slow death the fucking party of the decade."

"Your reputation precedes you, Crumdog."

CRUMDOG GAVE HIM THE name and address of a suitable motel in Needles and hung up. Pulling out of the parking lot, Rigby saw Jason the Tweaker across the street hopping up and down on his left leg and exhibiting such childlike delight he almost regretted what he'd told the Brewster. But he consoled himself with the knowledge that Jason's greed had cost him an extra ninety bucks at a moment when he could scarce afford to negotiate, and he didn't think about him again the whole way back to Ventura.

Heading up the 5, Rigby gunned it. He was saved. Stony Flynn, a former client who owed him a few favors and knew that his finances were shaky, had let him know that if he could procure two hundred grand in cash, there was an accountant in La Jolla with a desperate need to get rid of a great deal of purloined coke, worth a great deal more than the asking price. Stony hadn't meant to suggest that Rigby do the buying and selling himself, just thought he might supply the seed money and take a cut, but he underestimated both Rigby's taste for risk and the depth of his current financial woes. Another former client, a serial arsonist named Pooty Tang (known in court documents as Desmond Tutwiler), had a connection with the Devil's Hammers motorcycle club of Topeka, Kansas, and for a thousand-dollar bribe had arranged the introduction.

THAT AFTERNOON, RIGBY HAD met with the accountant in Carlsbad to make the exchange. He turned out to be a perspiration-soaked man with a tiny head in proportion to his body and a birdlike way of jerking his head around to check for threats. At the end of the meeting, he'd left the bar carrying the brand-new attaché Rigby had bought to hold the money and gone out to an old red Ford Focus and driven away. Neither knew the other's name.

And now there was two hundred thousand dollars' worth of uncut powder in the spare tire compartment, ready to convert into maybe half a million dollars without so much as cutting it. He couldn't wait to tell Paula. Of course, there was no need for her to know the details. Hell, she didn't know half of what had gone wrong in the last year and a half anyway. He'd managed to keep that from her; all she needed to know was that they were solvent again and weren't going to lose the house. He wasn't always a perfect husband, but when things got down and dirty, he always came through for her.

CHAPTER TWO

SHE WAS HALF AN hour early for a ten o'clock meeting with a client in an old house on Thompson, converted into a coffee shop with a wavy wooden floor and surly staff. With a black coffee and a Danish before her, she was optimistic about the prospect of catching up on some work emails when she looked up and, to her horror, saw Beth Warden striding toward her table. *Shit.*

"Paula," Beth said, her voice an octave higher than normal. "It's been forever."

She stood and forced a smile and accepted Beth's embrace, kissed her on the cheek and sat back down. "Just getting caught up on some business," she said.

Beth sat down as though she hadn't heard and took a sip of her drink. "How is everything?"

This loathsome woman controls a significant portion of your finances, and now is not the time to throw scalding coffee in her treacherous face or to stab her hand with your pastry fork, she told herself. *That day will come in the fullness of time.*

"Everything's great," she said, confident that the pleasant expression on her face read as genuine. Paula was nothing if not a consummate saleswoman. She looked down at her tablet and her phone and gestured. "I've got quite a bit to get through before my client gets here."

"The kids are running me ragged lately, between school and extracurriculars," Beth said, as though Paula had asked. "Hey, was Danny ever in the Boy Scouts?"

The woman could not take a hint. "He was for a while, through St. Anthony. He gave it up in middle school." Her phone rang, the vibrations making it dance on the table, and even though it was her boss, to whom she didn't want to speak, she picked up. "Germaine, hi, you were on my call list this morning." Until Beth had arrived, she hadn't told a lie all day.

"Funny, seemed like you were avoiding me."

"No, it's just been a crazy week. I'm just about to meet with a client and going through some messages, you know how you get behind." She gave Beth a sidelong glance.

"That's why I'm calling, I can't find the last of the paperwork on the Murray house. Did you get it filed?"

"Shit. This afternoon. Just as soon as I'm done with Dora Kenton. Before lunch."

"Okay, kid. I've never known you to let these things slide."

Once she hung up, she made a show of checking her emails rather than addressing Beth.

"You sure lead a busy life, Paula. I don't know how you do it." She reached across the table and put her hand on Paula's. "By the way, I'm starting a memorial scholarship at Third Presbyterian in Britt's name. I hope I can count on you for a thousand."

A thousand! Good God, the balls on the woman. "You'll have to ask Rigby, he makes all the decisions about those kinds of things."

"That doesn't sound like you, Paula, not very modern."

"Division of labor. Do you want me to have him call you, or do you just want to wait until you run into him?" Paula said this with her most ingenuous smile, as though she didn't know that Rigby and Beth met at least two or three times a week, mostly in the dark.

"Oh, I can call him, that's fine," she said.

Beth didn't shut up or stand until the client arrived. Paula then spent forty-five minutes going through listings they might tour, and out of the thirty they discussed came up with a short list of only five. Afterward, driving down Thompson, she mulled over the possibility of confiding in Germaine. They'd been friends for years, and the burden of not having anyone to tell her real troubles to was wearing her down slowly. No doubt part of her sales slump was connected to it. But to admit to Germaine the kind of debt they were in, how close they were to losing the house, the fact that Rigby's practice was down to a single client, that might actually make things worse. Instead of empathy for an old friend and protégée's plight, she might feel contempt and anger for being put into a situation where one of her top agents was getting foreclosed on. And Germaine had never liked Rigby, always made it quite clear that she saw through the charm right down to the lying, cheating bastard underneath. For years Paula had tried subtly to change her opinion, but over time she'd come to realize that the old girl was dead-on about her husband's character.

And now Rigby had some sort of cockamamie bullshit scheme, whose details he refused to share, that he claimed was going to pull the fat out of the fire and save the house. She didn't want to hear what Germaine would certainly have to say about that.

Halfway to the office she drove past a bus bench with her own beaming face on it. Why couldn't she live up to that stupid head shot? She pulled over to the curb and took her phone out of her purse.

Fuck it, I can tell Keith. Why not?

"Keith? Are you free this afternoon?"

"Got a lesson at one-thirty, I could meet you at three."

The boyish enthusiasm in his voice thrilled her. The hell with Germaine, and the hell with Rigby. She was going to get laid and forget about all of it that afternoon.

CHAPTER THREE

STAINED AMBER LIKE THE rest of the room's fixtures by decades of nicotine, an ancient beige window unit rattled and wheezed, pouring out tepid air that smelled of mildew, and its cycling on and off didn't seem to correspond to any actual changes in the room's temperature. Billy hadn't ever been to Needles before, and he hadn't expected it to be near this hot at the end of April. Past a hundred degrees before noon, the little guy who checked him in said, peering over drugstore reading glasses. Billy suspected the man had just pocketed the ninety dollars cash he'd given him, since he never saw the man fill out any paperwork.

He sat on the bed, waiting for a knock on the door and looking over the knapsack as though someone were right there in the room with him waiting to steal it. It was just Billy, though, alone in the room, still tweaking a little bit from the night before and thinking about what he was going to do with the five thousand he was going to get when this business was all done with. Buy some dope, obviously, but maybe also a down payment on a '78 Firebird Esprit he'd had his eye on. Or a deposit on a better apartment than he had so he could get Magda to move in with him. That shit about her living in Moorpark wasn't flying anymore, he was tired of making the drive all the time, and she wouldn't even set foot in his place anymore.

It was a real lucky break, Ernie setting him up with the lawyer. This was going to be the easiest five grand anybody ever made. Shit, the lawyer'd even given him two hundred in advance for gas, the motel and some food. He'd eaten dinner at Applebee's, splurging on a T-bone steak with seasoned fries and three giant draft beers. He'd congratulated himself for his cunning when the waitress asked to see his ID and he'd handed her his fake one, which he still kept at the age of twenty-three for just such an occasion. The lawyer was going to be proud of him when he heard about it. *No sir, I didn't want anybody in Needles knowing my real name.* He'd checked into the motel using the same driver's license, though that squirrely clerk had given it only the most perfunctory of glances. Warren Evans was the name on the card, with an address in Long Beach, and Billy's picture on it looked just like he imagined a Warren Evans would look, all serious and intense. It had cost him a hundred dollars when he was nineteen, from a guy who sold ID cameras and had a sideline making phony IDs for underage drinkers and other low-level miscreants.

He thought about what Magda was going to say when he pulled out the wad of bills and said here it is, baby, five thousand dollars cash, let's go spend some of this shit. First thing he was going to do was take her out for a nice dinner. Lobster, maybe, at the Sportsman downtown.

He wanted to masturbate, but he didn't know exactly when the guy was coming by, so it didn't seem like a good idea unless he could rub one out real quick, and without any visual aids it might take a while. The TV didn't even have premium channels, let alone Pay-Per-View smut, but he reasoned that when you were doing this kind of high-end shady business, you couldn't do it at a Holiday Inn or a Red Roof. In any case, he didn't want to do the handover sporting a boner.

It was ten forty-five when the knock finally came. Looking through the peephole, he saw a tall, lanky bald guy in leathers marked DEVIL'S HAMMERS TOPEKA. The fringes of his hair had grown to a considerable length, matching the fringes of his leathers, and Billy opened up.

He stood in the doorway and Billy tried to think of some way to make sure he was the actual guy and not some joker out to rob him, not so much because he thought that might be the case but because he didn't want to look like some corn-fed rube who didn't know any better. But he couldn't think of anything like that.

"Goddamn it, you gonna let me in or what?" the guy said.

"Sure," Billy said, and he stepped aside to let him pass.

"I'm Billy," he said once they were both inside with the door closed.

"I don't want to know your fuckin' name."

"Oh. Well, here it is, anyway." He opened up the brief-case, and the guy stuck a penknife into one of the packets and tasted the end of the blade with the tip of his pointy tongue.

"Yeah, seems all right to me, but I'm no expert. I'm going to have to take it to Barstow and let Crumdog have a taste. You got a problem with that?"

"Who's Crumdog?"

"Sergeant-at-Arms of the Devil's Hammers. He says the shit's what you say it is, I'll be back in, like, two hours with your cash."

The guy snapped the backpack closed, tucked it under his arm, gave him a happy little two-finger salute as he stepped outside, then hopped onto his hog and rode away. Billy felt pretty good. That was a lot of dope in that backpack, a lot more than he'd imagined, and it was exciting to be part of a big deal like this. He figured the lawyer might be using him from now on for more missions like this, might make him a trusted lieutenant or something. Now to sit back and wait for the guy to come back with the money.

CHAPTER FOUR

"JERRY, IT'S SO GREAT to see you," a woman's voice said, and a hand clutched on his right elbow.

He tensed and grinned, both ends of his mouth open while his lips touched in the center. He was aware that this was a silly expression, but it was his natural smile of surprise and beyond his control. The grin intensified when he realized who was addressing him. She smelled wonderful, too, a scent redolent of Meyer lemons and springtime.

"Oh, Belinda, huh, hi, nice to see you." He felt his face reddening and tried to control the smile. She was petite, her auburn hair in a bob, lipstick a vivid glossy orange, and she inspired in Jerry a strong urge to do something foolish and socially ruinous. He wished he had the nerve to try some such thing, because he hated these charity events more now than he ever had before. The sympathetic looks of those who pitied him was worse than the contempt of those who snickered, and the humiliation of turning up alone—a necessity lately, since he couldn't afford to properly escort a woman of his own social class—made it worse. Not buying a ticket would be unthinkable, but buying two would be an inexcusable extravagance in his current financial state.

"I just got up to fetch a drink between lots. You buy anything?" Her dress was aquamarine, made of some shiny fabric that looked like it would be soft to the touch, its hem well above Belinda's lovely knees. Why were the women who moved him the most always the married ones?

"Ah, no. Haven't even bid." He didn't add that this was out of fear that he wouldn't be outbid.

"I wish Trey hadn't! He paid eight hundred dollars for a charcoal drawing of a horse that looks like a ten-year-old drew it."

"Oh, that one. Yeah, I saw that. Good for the school, though."

"I know, it's a good cause. Still." She put a hand to her hip and jutted it rightward. "Where are you sitting?"

"I got up after the dinner was finished. I didn't know anyone at my table."

She put her arm through his and pulled him with her. "Come on, sit next to me, we've got room. Besides, Trey'll want to say hi."

"Sure," he said, not at all sure he wanted to see Trey in Belinda's presence. It was all he could manage at the moment not to stare down the top of her dress.

"I want to get another drink first," she said. "You want one?"

He sensed that she'd already had more than was her usual, and he thrilled to the notion that it might make her adventuresome and reckless. Maybe they could ditch the banquet and check into a room upstairs. Or maybe they could just screw behind a curtain in one of the empty meeting rooms.

He forced his thoughts back to reality. "Gin and tonic, thanks."

"You're so sweet. We're at table six, close to the auctioneer. Is he the worst ever or what?"

"He's not very good."

She laughed as hard as if he'd just said something very funny, and he hurried to the table before his erection got any worse.

Trey was drunker than Belinda, and he kept slapping Jerry between the shoulder blades. "You know the Kimballs?" he said, waving his hand at the couple across the table.

"You just introduced us," he said.

The Kimballs, who looked too young to have kids old enough to be enrolled at Creston Prep, exchanged uncomfortable glances.

"Did I? Well, I'm one polite son of a bitch."

Mrs. Kimball had long, straight, dark brown hair and pale, worried eyes. She leaned forward and spoke slowly.

"Trey, you've had quite a bit to drink," she said.

"Damn right I have."

"So has Belinda."

"Oh, hell, Belinda hasn't even started yet. When she gets a load on, you'll know it."

Mrs. Kimball looked back at her husband. He had the earnest look of a high school guidance counselor, and before he spoke he stood.

"Kelly and I don't think either one of you should drive home tonight."

Trey waved off the foolish notion with a swat of his hand. "Belinda will drive, she does it all the time."

He saw Belinda just then, weaving her way through the crowd with a cardboard drink tray. She did look fairly plastered at that, more so than he'd noticed earlier.

Trey slapped his back again. "Me and Jerry, senior year, remember this, Jer? We led the cops on a merry chase through Maplewood all the way down to Rock Hill, they finally stopped us with a spike strip. Well, we spent the night in the drunk tank, and in the morning it was Jerry's uncle who got us out of there. I don't know how much it cost him, but it was a lot. I got off with a fucking speeding ticket! Try getting away with that shit today."

Belinda set a gin and tonic in a clear plastic goblet down next to Jerry and leaned down to give him a wet, sloppy kiss on the right cheek. He was glad he was sitting down with his lap obscured by the table cloth.

"You better watch out, Trey, I might just dump you for Jerry," she said. "He appreciates a woman." God, she did sound drunk now. Had she chugged another one at the cash bar?

"Be my guest, pal," Trey said, elbowing Jerry. "Pain in the ass."

"Are you going to let him talk about me that way, Jerry?"

The Kimballs were staring now. "Don't pay any mind," Jerry said. "We go way back and they're always teasing me."

"We do go way back. My old man was actually pretty pissed off at your uncle Glenn for bailing us out, can you imagine that? Thought we should have taken our lumps. 'Course back then a DUI wasn't as serious a thing as now, but still. How is old Glenn, anyway?"

"He's got his health problems, but I guess he's okay."

Trey pointed to the Kimballs. "You guys won't believe who his uncle is. Ever watch *Kilgore, MD*? Remember that show?"

Mr. Kimball was still standing. "I'm serious about this, Trey. We'll pay for a cab."

"Cab? That's pretty old school. It's Uber now."

"Fine, we'll gladly pay for an Uber." Kimball sat down again, not entirely certain whether he'd won the argument or not.

"Fuck it, I just spent eight hundred on a drawing, I can afford my own Uber. Listen, though, *Kilgore*? Medical show, set in a Detroit charity ward? Or *High Cimarron*? About the widow rancher and her sons?"

Kelly Kimball spoke again. "I've seen that on reruns."

"Yeah, right? That was Jerry's uncle Glenn, one of the biggest TV producers there was back in the day. Jerry's dad's brother."

Mr. Kimball brightened. "Is that Glenn Haskill? We've been talking to him about a bequest."

Jerry, not very interested in the Kimballs up to this point, perked up. "Really?"

"Yes, and he was the one who contacted us. We didn't even have him listed in our alumni database."

"I'm sorry, I didn't catch your first name?"

Kimball stood back up and reached across the table to shake his hand. "I'm sorry, it's Wells Kimball, assistant director of development."

"What sort of a bequest?"

"He's still figuring it out with his attorney."

Rigby. That sleazy son of a bitch. Jerry'd have to work his way into the equation somehow, make damned sure the whole estate wasn't going to the school. And why was this even a consideration? Uncle Glenn had never made any secret of his hatred of the school.

Onstage, the auctioneer was lamenting the inattention of the crowd, more intent on after-dinner conversation than the auction. On offer was a trip for five to the Bahamas, and only three bids had been registered, the last for a mere eight thousand dollars. "Come on, folks, it would be a real shame if this went for such a low bid. Do I hear eight thousand five hundred?"

"Fuck it," Belinda said, and raised her placard. "Nine thousand!"

"Nine thousand," the auctioneer shouted. "Nine thousand from table six!"

"Who gives a shit, right?" she said to Jerry, leaning in. "It's only money, right?"

Wells Kimball looked at his phone. "Jerry, I don't have you in my contacts. The school has your info, right?"

"Oh, you've definitely got it." Barely a week went by without a plea for funds in the mail. Apart from tickets to auctions and garage sales, he hadn't given the school a dime in ten years.

"Are you related to Valerie Haskill?"

"She's my ex-wife."

Kimball seemed pleased. "Valerie's been very generous over the last five years."

What the hell was that about? She'd never attended the school, never shown any particular interest in it, rarely attended any functions. But she was making generous donations? And presumably out of the alimony that was such a factor in keeping him in the red.

"Maybe you could come in one morning and we could have a chat," Kimball said.

"My charitable giving is pretty well set at this point. When did you say my uncle contacted you?"

"Not long after the first of the year. He seems very alert for a man of his age."

Someone else bid nine thousand five hundred on the Bahamas trip. "Do I hear ten thousand?"

"Eleven thousand!" Belinda yelled, waving her placard above her head.

"Goddamn it, that's not the way bidding works, Belinda," Trey said, grabbing for the placard, which she yanked out of his reach with a cackle.

"Screw you, I'm going to the Bahamas." She threaded her arm through Jerry's elbow and clutched his hand. "Jerry wouldn't try to stop me if I were his wife."

The news about Uncle Glenn was so alarming he couldn't even enjoy the attention from Belinda. "The thing is, Wells," Jerry said, "Uncle Glenn's not in good shape, mentally. Sometimes he gives things away and doesn't remember. And of course that leads to problems because he thinks he's been robbed."

Kimball nodded, frowning. "Of course, this will all be done through his attorney, with all the relevant paperwork signed, sealed, et cetera."

Belinda let go of Jerry and stood up, then walked around him to Trey.

"Sure, sure. Just wanted to make sure you understood."

Now she was hissing something into Trey's ear, and Trey hissed something equally incomprehensible into hers. She sat down on his lap and he kissed her, and then they were making out like teenagers.

Someone else bid eleven thousand two hundred fifty, and after a long, painful attempt to attract another bid, the gavel went down. "Sold, to the lady at table nineteen for eleven thousand, two hundred fifty dollars," the auctioneer said, heartbroken.

Belinda got up from Trey's lap. "You asshole! You kissed me on purpose, just to keep me from winning!"

Trey shrugged. "Sue me," he said, and the look on Belinda's face was one of lustful adoration.

CHAPTER FIVE

THE SHARP SMELL OF mold made Rigby's sinuses burn something fierce, and he felt the stirrings of what promised to be an agonizing headache. He stood across from Billy Knox at the latter's dismal, tiny crib on Ventura Avenue, failing to grasp more than the broadest outlines of the story the glue-addled little turdbucket was trying to get across.

"What happened to the money, Billy?"

Knox was confused, his acned forehead contorted into knots of unaccustomed concentration. "Nothing happened to the money."

"Then why aren't you giving me the money?"

"Because I don't have it?" He seemed to think he'd explained all this sufficiently already, and he winced as if in anticipation of a blow. Knox Senior must either have hit little Billy too often growing up or not often enough, Rigby thought.

"All right. You don't have the money. Where's the product?"

"The product?"

Jesus. When they'd met in the Shanty, Knox had given off an air of sullen, taciturn badassery so pure it hadn't occurred to Rigby that he might be enlisting a certified moron to assist him in the commission of a serious felony.

He'd been almost scared of the little man at the time, so convincing was his mien of barely suppressed violence. Now that the shit-for-brains was finally speaking more than three words at a time, Rigby understood that he'd torpedoed the whole operation, just by trusting his gut and not digging deeper. "The backpack you had with you."

"Oh. The dope, you mean?"

Now Rigby winced. It was his practice to avoid saying potentially troublesome words out loud. "That's it, Billy. Where is it?"

"Those Devil Hammers got it."

"Did they rob you?"

"No, sir. They took it with them like they were supposed to."

"Then what happened to the money?"

Knox looked up at Rigby as if considering the possibility that he was just being fucked with for a laugh. "Already told you, nothing happened."

"Then give me the money." Rigby was aware of an increasing edge in his tone of voice, a threat of violence that he didn't really mean to project. But if this fuckwit didn't start talking sense in about thirty seconds, he wasn't sure he'd be able to resist the urge to beat the fuck right out of him.

"I don't have it! They never came back!"

A dim light began to dawn in Rigby's brain. He had failed to understand Billy Knox's story because he had failed to appreciate the pure, sublime depth of his stupidity. "So you're telling me you gave them the product and allowed them to leave without paying first?"

"He said he had to take it back to this one guy for a taste, then he'd come back and settle."

The sure knowledge that he'd been robbed settled on him and clung like a shroud. He accepted it and pressed ahead with his dim interlocutor. "And you're sitting there in the motel room in Needles waiting for them to come back for how long?"

"Waited till this morning, then thought I should get back and tell you." He swelled momentarily with pride. "I remembered you didn't want me using my phone up there, calling you, 'cause the five-o might trace it."

Rigby shook his head in disbelief at his own idiocy. He'd thought of himself as being smarter than the average bear. He wouldn't do the dirty, direct part of it himself, he'd decided. Instead, he'd hire a mean motherfucker to do it, a man on the wrong side of the law: an outlaw, to be sure, but also a man with a code. He should have administered an IQ test instead. "Well, there, Billy, that was a very smart move on your part. Not phoning me, just hightailing it back down here." The rage that had been building earlier was gone now, replaced by an eerie calm. "Why do you guess they needed to leave for a taste?"

"I guess their Secretary of the Army needed to taste it first, and he wasn't there in the room."

"Sergeant-at-Arms," he said, resisting the temptation to add "you dumb fuck." Rigby was blaming himself now. The half-hour's worth of conversation with the dolt the night before he sent him out should have revealed the limits of Knox's intellect; Rigby's own lack of criminal experience had fucked him.

"Crumdog's what he called the guy. Seemed kind of scared of him. I sure could understand how he'd want the guy to make sure they didn't get burned."

Visions of bankruptcy, disbarment, divorce and prison pinwheeled in Rigby's mind. He could maybe stay afloat until old Glenn Haskill died, but that wouldn't be long, and once it happened they'd be looking at all his accounts. Even with Haskill's kind of money, two hundred grand was a large amount to go missing.

It was his own fault, though, not Knox's; there was no use blaming a mentally handicapped guy for behaving like a mentally handicapped guy. "I guess we're done here, then."

"Uh, except one thing. Where's my five grand?"

"Excuse me?" Surely he jested! Who would have expected a pinhead to have a sense of humor?

"The five grand you owe me, I'll take it now."

"The five grand I was going to pay you before you lost my—" He stopped himself before saying the word out loud. "My backpack. See, you don't get the five grand because that was going to be your share of the money, and there's no money because you let yourself get ripped off."

Head cocked boldly to one side, Knox no longer seemed afraid of Rigby. Maybe the notion of being owed money was making him brave. "No, sir, that's not the way I see it. You were going to pay me five grand. I didn't hear nothing about a share of anything."

"Let me explain something, Billy," he said, both hands tingling, his face getting hot. "You fucked up my deal so badly I may never recover. You cost me as much money as you see in ten years. You're getting jack shit."

"You know what I call that? I call that not being a man of honor. Might be I'll just have to go see John Law my own self. Tell 'em you ripped me off, motherfucker."

It happened before he was consciously aware of it: right fist forming, right arm cocking back, then shooting forward into Knox's jaw with a loud crunching sound, followed milliseconds later by a pitiful animal wail of pain and self-pity. Knox was on the floor, his face contorted like that of a six-year-old who's just fallen off a jungle gym onto concrete.

"Think I broke your jaw there, Billy."

Billy hollered something unintelligible, probably either a threat of vengeance or a plea for medical assistance, or maybe some combination thereof. He was spitting blood, and only now did Rigby notice that his hand hurt, too. That was a pretty good punch, he thought, not without a hint of the sin of pride.

HEADING HOME, HE CONSIDERED the degree to which the sock on Knox's jaw had lightened his mood. Just for that moment, he felt pretty wonderful. All he had to do was come up with a couple hundred grand before Glenn Haskill went tits up and he'd be fine.

He had, he reflected, a great deal to be grateful for. A beautiful wife, sexier at forty-two than on the day they'd met, three wonderful kids, a lot of terrific friends and a certain standing in the community. He was banging his late partner's smoking-hot widow on practically a daily basis, and she didn't even want him to leave Paula.

Speaking of which, why not stop by Beth's house for a quickie? She wouldn't appreciate the short notice, but her kids would be asleep by now. He had a bottle of twenty-year-old Balvenie in the trunk as an offering. Pity it was a good bottle; Beth's affections could be bought for Chivas Regal, whereas his wife wouldn't settle for a bribe short of single malt.

The booze would earn him some goodwill, though, at least enough for a blow job, maybe the whole deal if he was charming enough or she got loopy enough. He'd had an extraordinarily shitty day, and though he couldn't share with her the details, he knew she'd want to make it better.

BETH WAS KIND OF a bitch about being phoned awake at one-thirty on a weeknight, though as Rigby was quick to point out, she didn't have a job. All she had to do in the morning was get up and oversee the nanny taking her kids to school, whereas Rigby had a law practice to run practically single-handedly. This last was a cruel but necessary guilt trip on Rigby's part. It was a plain fact, though, that if Beth's husband hadn't checked out of the land of the upright in the stupidest accident Rigby ever heard of, he wouldn't be in the position he was in at the moment—to wit, stealing from the one rich client the firm had left. He left out the part about the stealing, naturally, but he knew Beth felt bad about what had happened to the firm since Britt's death.

"All right," she said. "An hour, that's all you get. Bring a bottle."

SHE SIPPED AT THE Balvenie, smiling in the feline way she had when she'd had too much to drink, which meant she'd probably already emptied half a bottle before she went to bed. They were drinking on the sofa in her bedroom, and he noted that she'd made the bed since he called and woke her. Presentation was everything.

"You're bad, getting me out of bed at this hour on a school night. What are you doing out so late?"

One of the things Rigby really hated was people asking him questions the answers to which were none of their fucking business. "I was at the office trying to make sense of some numbers." How was that for meaningless?

"Numbers. Well."

She was fully made up, too, short blond hair perfectly coiffed, wearing a blue silk nightdress he liked, and he hoped it wouldn't take long to coax her out of it. All he really wanted was a quick orgasm to wash the toxins out of his brain and body. He lunged for her, hoping she'd respond and let him have what he wanted so he could go home and sleep.

"Jesus, Rigby, you're such a pig," she said, but there was guttural pleasure in it, and soon enough the nightdress was on the floor, the bed unmade again as he ground away inside her, listening to her repertoire of sex noises, throaty grunts and high-pitched sighs. She moved swiftly enough between one and the next that he knew she, too, expected it to be quick. He finished with what would have been a loud moan if not for the need to keep his presence a secret from her kids—it was a clenched growl instead, after which he pulled out and fell down on the sheets next to her.

Of course, the first thing he thought about afterward was his old pal Britt. He hardly ever got to screw Beth at the house because of kids and neighbors, but for Rigby, part of the thrill and repulsion of her bedroom was his inescapable sense there that Britt was witness to their posthumous betrayal. *Hope you weren't watching, pal.* Mea culpa!

ONCE HOME, HE SHOWERED and slipped into bed next to Paula, careful not to wake her. She smelled so good he started to get hard again and he nearly woke her, but thought better of it and rolled over to go to sleep. No need to be greedy.

She stirred and reached out for his forearm. "Where you been?"

"Saw a man about a horse."

"That's nice," she mumbled. Her lack of interest in the truth filled him with a rare, sentimental burst of fondness, and the urge to confess—partially, anyway—manifested itself.

"Babe, that deal I didn't exactly tell you about?"

"Mmm."

"When I said don't worry, I got cash coming through?"

He turned on the lamp on his side of the bed and she sat up, leaning on her right elbow, squinting at him. "Yeah?"

"Well, I just got royally fucked. I mean royally, baby. And the seed money came out of Haskill's account."

She was wide awake now. "My God. Okay. Don't panic. How likely is Haskill to notice?" she asked. Then, after a thoughtful pause: "Can you take any more?"

He caressed her cheek with the back of his hand. Bless her naïve, black little heart.

CHAPTER SIX

SHE WAS WAITING IN front of the house on Channel Drive when the phone rang. She wouldn't have picked up, but her clients were late and she'd finished her newspaper.

"Paula? It's Mom."

"I know it is. What's up?"

"Nothing's up, why does something have to be up? What are you doing?"

"Sitting in the car, waiting to show a client a house."

"How's Danny? Is he out of school yet?"

"Another few weeks. The girls are fine, too, thanks for asking."

"Oh, stop it, I was just about to ask about them. I don't play favorites with my grandchildren."

"What's Danny's birthday?"

"March fourteenth."

"What's the girls' birthday?"

"Please. You think I don't know?"

"What is it?"

"September third."

"It's September fifth."

"Like I've ever missed one in twelve years. Anyway, I did want to tell you something exciting. It seems Kyle's finally met a girl."

"Seems to me he knows plenty of girls."

"I mean someone he's interested in. He told me."

"Kyle's messing with you, Mom."

"You think you know everything about everyone, Paula. Why don't you think she could be a girlfriend?"

"What makes you think she could be a girlfriend?"

"Well, they work together at the school, and it sure does sound like they're spending a lot of time together. Her name is Rebecca."

"Okay."

"Maybe he'll marry her and Wayne can finally move out."

"Mom, you know Wayne and Kyle own that house together, right?"

"Well, Kyle could buy him out. Or the other way around. Maybe she could introduce Wayne to a girl."

"You know, Mom, some days I have the patience to humor you and some days I don't."

"Humor me? Please."

"Kyle and Wayne have been roommates since grad school. Kyle turned forty-two last year. They own real estate jointly. Neither of them has ever had a girlfriend. They have mailing labels with both their names on them."

"You're disgusting, trying to turn their friendship into something ugly."

"It's not ugly, Mom, it's perfectly normal."

"Paula, if your brother were homosexual, I'm sure he would have told me years ago. At least after your father died."

"Okay, Mom, let's move on."

"Do you think it runs in families?"

"I don't know."

"You never met my uncle Chet. Grandpa's little brother."

"The one who got run over?"

"Hit by a streetcar. In San Francisco, if you get my meaning."

"No, I don't."

"I think you do. He was a florist. And he moved from Ohio to San Francisco. And after he was killed by the streetcar, there was just a memorial service. No mass."

"Okay. I'd say the preponderance of evidence points to him being gay. Not an easy thing for someone in his generation."

"So if it were true, not just about Chet, but your brother, too?"

"Uh-huh?"

"Would that make it likely that Danny might be also?"

"Danny? I promise you have nothing to worry about on that score."

"Because it's a terrible sin, Paula."

"Okay, listen, Mom, I gotta go, my clients just pulled up. Love you."

She hung up, the clients nowhere in sight. Every year or two, her mother came up with an imaginary girlfriend for her brother in the nebulous vein of this Rebecca. Now that she was getting on, these fantasies were popping up more frequently.

The funny part of it was that her mother could be a very astute judge of character. When she'd first brought Rigby home, her father and everyone else in the family thought he was a swell fellow, but her mother had seen something dodgy about him right away. And now, after twenty years of marital osmosis, there was something dodgy about Paula, too.

The old girl was wrong to worry about Danny, who took after his father. A couple of months earlier, after she and Rigby and the girls had spent the weekend in San Diego without him, she'd come across a condom and a pair of panties in his bedsheets, the former item coming as a relief.

And now the nine o'clock clients pulled up in front of

her. They were relocating from Indianapolis for the wife's new job in Santa Monica, an hour and a half south of town on the best of days, which were rare. When she and Rigby had first arrived, the idea of Ventura as a bedroom community for Angelenos was still met with resistant disbelief; these days, though, it was considered an acceptable commute from west LA.

So far, they hadn't liked anything. She didn't expect them to like this one either, a classic 1920s bungalow, stucco with a detached garage and a decent-sized backyard, but something clicked with them as soon as they pulled up in front of it. The husband, normally silent to the point of sullenness, kept asking his wife what she thought, while she kept oohing and aahing over features that Paula had shown them in half a dozen other, better houses. Maybe it was the fact that the house, unoccupied for over two years, was completely empty, the client having ignored his realtor's suggestion that they hire a staging company to give a sense of what the house would look like occupied. The unfortunate realtor was a friend of Paula's, and she only brought the Handys over as a favor to said friend, who had begun to despair of ever unloading the property.

"The price is all right," Becki Handy said.

"They'd probably go down a little bit. It's been on the market for a while."

Shane Handy shook his disproportionately large head. He had a very black, very pointed chin beard that contrasted with the sweaty alabaster of his face. "We'll pay the asking."

Jesus Christ. "Let's not get ahead of ourselves," she said. "Now I have to tell you a few things about the house, why it's been empty for a while. The previous owner took his own life in the master bedroom. He hanged himself from that exposed beam."

The Handys looked in one another's eyes for a moment, then back at Paula. "We're good with that," Becki said, the picture of dull equanimity.

"They didn't find him for over a week, he was estranged from his family, and they had to replace the carpet and the hardwood underneath," she said, leaving out the fact that her friend swore she could still detect an atavistically horrifying trace of odor in that room, despite the thousands of dollars' worth of professional cleaning that went into making the place sellable. Paula smelled nothing and suspected that the poor woman was a victim of the power of suggestion, having spent too many hours devoted to the house and its myriad horrors.

"If they cleaned it up I don't see what the problem would be," said Shane.

"Of course not," Paula said, and despite the fact that she needed the sale, and that she would dearly love to be rid of the Handys, she felt an irrational resistance to letting them buy this house. "There's more, though."

She found herself resenting the Handys' bovine indifference more bitterly than before. They looked at each other once again and smirked in unison, and impulsively she hauled out the big guns, as Cheryl would have to do eventually before any paperwork went through.

"It's not just the old man's suicide that makes the place a hard sell. Before he put the place on the market his grandson decided to demolish the toolshed in the backyard."

"No toolshed? Damn. That's a deal killer," Shane brayed, and he and Becki both erupted in mirthless, hostile laughter, as though what she was telling them couldn't possibly be enough to disrupt their incipient love affair with this charming little charnel house.

Both of them still smirking, Paula kept a perfectly straight face, taking care to express neither amusement nor irritation in her tone as she continued. "When the handyman knocking it down got to the cement foundation, which he thought was odd, he found a handmade cedar chest underneath. He called the grandson in case it was something valuable. That shed had been up for forty years at least, and when they opened it up it had a canvas bag full of old gray bones." For the first time it struck her that she knew this story in greater detail than might be considered normal for someone unconnected with it. "Including a human skull."

"Ew. I'm glad they took that shed down before we bought it, then." Becki made a little moue of distaste, then giggled.

"The dead man's wife had supposedly up and left him without warning in 1969. That struck everyone as weird back then, because she left three kids behind, all of them in grade school. Husband said she met another man, ran away with him, and everyone believed it."

"So now it's solved. I don't see how that affects the property value," Shane said.

Of course you wouldn't, because you're a sociopath. If you weren't, you'd know better than to wear that fucking Van Dyke. "None of the kids had easy lives afterward. The only one who did all right was the grandson's father. He finally quit drinking and made a good living selling orthopedic shoes until he got killed at a railroad crossing." The details were pure invention at this point, but their indifference to the house's past infuriated her.

"Seriously, Paula, these kinds of things don't bother us." Becki was staring at the ceiling in the front parlor, which had a low crossbeam just like the deadly one in the master bedroom. "Let's make an offer."

CHAPTER SEVEN

AFTER BREAKFAST, RIGBY HEADED south on the 101 to Oxnard. Breaking Billy Knox's jaw was a thing he felt the need to confess immediately, as opposed to the sort of peccadillo that could wait for Sunday morning with Paula and the kids. The past few years, he'd been going to confession in Camarillo on occasions such as these, or Santa Barbara or even further afield; he didn't want his parish priest in Ventura to know when he'd committed some especially shameful act, the kind of thing that made him want to get absolution in a hurry in case he got hit by a semi.

The priest hearing confession in the little church in Oxnard was young, Latino and soft-spoken; in addition to breaking Knox's jaw, Rigby had a couple of small, garden-variety sins he needed to get off his chest, so he started with those.

"I had intercourse, sexual, with a lady other than my wife, twice this week. The other lady isn't married, she's a widow," he said, not sure whether that made any difference in terms of his own culpability, adultery-wise. "I also masturbated three times to thoughts of a woman who is also, uh, not my wife. And I lost my temper and yelled out my car window at a little old lady who was driving too slow. Cursed at her, called her a cunt—sorry, Padre. And, uh, I hurt a guy pretty badly."

"Hurt him in what way?"

"I broke his jaw with my fist, Father. For which I'm heartily sorry."

The priest paused for an uncomfortably long moment. "What was your reason for hitting this man?"

Fuck me, I had to go and pick a priest who wants a whole entertaining anecdote. "Well, father, the truth of the matter is, he was supposed to do some work for me and he messed it up real bad, and I lost my temper." He hoped it was all right to leave out the nature of the work Knox was supposed to have done for him.

The priest sighed and started laying out Rigby's penance.

TEN MINUTES LATER, HE stood in the afternoon sun, grousing under his breath. The young priest seemed to think Rigby had nothing better to do than say the rosary all goddamn day long, and this, he told himself, was the last time he was coming down here for confession. Not when old Father Dunbar up in Santa Barbara found his amatory exploits so entertaining. Dunbar was a priest of the old school who understood the kinds of trouble men got up to in the course of being men, so his penances for adultery weren't too stiff, as long as you gave him the details.

IT MADE HIM NERVOUS, but he decided to make the call. There was always the chance—a pretty good one, now that he considered it—that poor dim-witted Billy had just misread the situation, and that the Devil's Hammers were at that very moment trying to get him his money. He punched the number into the little burner flip phone and waited.

"Yo, Crumdog's phone."

"Let me talk to Crumdog."

"Fuck is this?"

"Lancer."

There was a silence, and then laughter. "Man, you don't want to talk to Crumdog."

"I promise you I do."

More laughter. "All right, man. Hold on."

"Lancer?" Crumdog sounded surprised.

"Crumdog."

"The fuck you want?"

"I got a confusing story from my man in Needles."

"Yeah? Confusing how, exactly?"

"He said your man took the material off for testing and never came back with the money."

"What I believe my lieutenant told your bitch is, he'd be back in a couple hours if—*if*—it was what you said."

"You saying it wasn't?"

"What do you think I'm saying?"

"You're saying it wasn't what I was told it was?"

"Listen, Lancer, we could keep playing Abbott and Costello all day long here, but let me lay it out for you. Your bitch gave my lieutenant the whole backpack, not just a taste. That was his bad and yours. If he hadn't you'd still have ninety percent of it, good or bad. I'm telling you I did you a favor and destroyed your plastic bricks of baby laxative. I'm doing you an even bigger favor by giving you the benefit of the doubt and assuming that you were just stupid and not actually trying to fuck me. Because I trust you understand the implications of the latter situation."

Rigby bristled at the man's tone and it fed his nerve. "How do I know you didn't just rob me blind?"

Crumdog laughed. "You don't know that at all. You got balls, Lancer, I'll give you that. But just in case you get a wild hair up your ass and decide to go to the DEA or the FBI or who the fuck ever you feel like appealing to for recourse, let me tell you something. Your name's not Lancer, it's Douglas

Rigby, attorney-at-law. You live on Via Cielito Street in Ventura, California. Your wife Paula's a realtor. Want me to keep going?"

"Not really."

"Listen, Rigby, I know it's gotta hurt, but you got fucked. Don't matter whether it was me stealing real product or some other asshole selling you fake, you just took a royal ass-fucking. I'm going to give you some good advice now: chalk it up to experience and forget you ever heard of me."

The line went dead and Rigby considered his options, the only viable one being to follow Crumdog's advice. Now that the possibility of recovering Glenn Haskill's money had vanished completely, though, he felt counterintuitively unburdened. He now faced the well-nigh impossible task of returning that money to the account before the Grim Reaper finally arrived for the old bastard, or else come up with a way to convincingly hide its theft. And in either case, he and Paula were still in deep financial shit. But there was something about the undeniable direness of the situation that stimulated him. His sense of self had always been that of an overmatched fighter, thriving in hopeless situations. He felt more confident and alive than he had when he'd first taken possession of the cocaine. Or whatever it had been.

CHAPTER EIGHT

RIGBY CAME HOME FOR lunch for once, his shaky
demeanor from the night before considerably smoother.
"Don't worry about it, baby. It's under control."

"We could lose the house, Rigby. That's a disaster for anybody, but for a real estate agent . . . Jesus, I don't even want
to think about it."

"Baby, did I just say I've got it under control or didn't
I?" He was squirting sriracha sauce onto a plate of cottage
cheese.

"You did, and as usual you left out the important details.
All the details, in fact. And also the broad strokes."

He took in a mouthful before he started to speak. "No
point in telling you at this stage, see?"

"Don't blow smoke up my ass. How much trouble are we
really in?"

He shrugged and made a face, eating fast and talking with
his mouth full of pinkish, mushy curds. "Look, we're not out
of it yet, but I've got a plan. We're going to be fine. Now, all
I need is for you to stop worrying." He finished the cottage
cheese and dropped the plate in the sink. "I'll be home late
tonight. Heading for Santa Barbara, going to have dinner
with Glenn."

Right, and then he was going to come back to Ventura
and fuck Beth. Sometimes it got to her, how stupid he took

her to be. As soon as he was out the garage door, she got on the phone.

A COUPLE OF HOURS later her eyes were closed, concentrating on the elusive promise of an orgasm as young Keith lapped away below. His noisy slurps were distracting, but a fair trade-off, she supposed, for the gusto he brought to the task. She arched her back, turned her head to the left toward the bedroom door, craned her neck, and just as she felt the thing starting to rise up through her nervous system, she opened her eyes just a sliver. There in the doorway was Stanley, a mangy, smelly, slightly damp sheepdog, his giant pink-and-black tongue lolling rhythmically and more or less in time with Keith's, and she let out a loud snort of a laugh that coincided with the orgasm and outlasted it. It returned intermittently while he fucked her, which didn't appear to bother him.

"TWO AFTERNOONS IN A row," Keith said afterward, lying naked on the top sheet, staring up at the ceiling with a simple, happy grin. "First time."

"Don't get any ideas. We still have to be careful as hell." Telling him her woes the day before had had its cathartic element, but there was a troubling change in his demeanor now that he knew a few secrets, as though listening to a few of her intimate troubles had earned him some kind of emotional intimacy. She'd assumed that sleeping with someone horny and young would allow her to steer clear of any kind of emotional involvement, but here was Keith, avid and puppyish and wanting her to be crazy about him in return.

As it happened, Keith knew the story of the murder house well, located as it was two short blocks from his grandfather's house. One of the murderer's grandsons had been in school a year ahead of Keith, probably the one who'd ordered the demolition of the shed, and children whispered then, as children will, about the long-ago disappearance of the boy's grandmother. "I followed it pretty close in the paper after they knocked down the shed and found that skeleton," he said. "I bet you could take a backhoe to that property and find a few more."

"I shouldn't care, should I? I should be happy to be rid of them and happy for my friend getting the house off her hands. But I swear to God, I can't stand the idea of those idiots buying it. Why is that, you think?"

"I don't know," Keith said. "Just think about the money. And you won't have to deal with them anymore."

Keith didn't think in complicated terms, one of the reasons she liked being around him. Her only other sounding board was Rigby, and half the time the son of a bitch didn't listen to what she was saying. "Maybe it's this," she said. "The husband, he's got this pointy black beard. I think he dyes it, and the wife is always making this creepy noise with her sinuses that sounds kind of like a snicker. They seem like Satanists or something."

"Satanists have to live somewhere, I guess."

"I mean, they almost seemed excited by the idea that the house was the site of a suicide and probably at least one murder way back."

"So you think they're going to commit more just because the house has such a good murder vibe?"

She started laughing again, partly because she found the phrase funny and partly because he'd nailed the source of her unfounded anxiety. The juxtaposition of the murder house and the Handys' creepiness had led her to construct for them an entirely new identity as a pair of perverted, murderous psychopaths instead of the socially awkward dullards they almost certainly were.

As Keith basked in the glory of having made her laugh, which seemed to please him more than having made her come, she started getting dressed. They'd been making use of his fellow pro Mickey's house for almost two weeks while Keith house-sat, feeding the dogs and watering the plants in return for a fuckpad that was relatively nice when you considered that its usual occupant was a single twenty-seven-year-old ex-frat rat of an assistant golf pro. "I wish your friend weren't coming back, this has been nice."

"I could clean my place up, make it nice."

She'd been there once and only once, and knew for a fact that nothing short of a bulldozer could turn Keith's skanky bachelor pad into a place she'd be willing to have sexual intercourse in, but she phrased her response carefully. "Your front door's visible from the street. Unlike your friend's."

"So?"

"So my face is on bus benches in this town. People know who I am, I can't be seen going in and out of some guy's apartment."

"You sure I couldn't clean it up?"

"It'll be fine, sweetie, we'll go back to empty houses. It'll be fun." She had a sudden desire for a cigarette. "Mickey doesn't smoke, does he?"

Keith looked as though she'd asked whether Mickey had sex with animals. "No," he said.

"Would he mind if I smoked in here?"

"You smoke?"

He looked so disappointed in her she was sorry she'd said anything. "Not really for years. Just sometimes I want one, and I can't smoke at home because Rigby'd freak, and it's Southern California so I can't ever have one in public. I don't have a pack, anyway. Rigby goes through my purse when he needs cash."

"Sorry. None of my beeswax."

She fixed her gaze on a pattern in the popcorn ceiling. "Am I prettier horizontal than vertical?"

"Beg pardon?"

"When you hit a certain age and you lie down on your back, you get kind of a gravitational face-lift. I was just wondering how much better I look that way."

"You look good either way."

"Hm. Well, every so often I look at myself and wonder if it isn't getting to be time."

"Time for what?"

"A face-lift."

"You're just fishing for compliments now."

"I'm serious."

"That's crazy. Those things don't look right. You know one of my clients who had one? Kathleen Fullerton. Look at her, eyes popping out of her sockets. And she wasn't half bad looking before that."

"Right, Rigby calls her 'Our Lady of Perpetual Surprise.' I'd certainly want a better surgeon than hers."

They retreated into silence while they dressed, and when the sheepdog came panting back into the room she felt a little sad.

DANNY SLURPED HIS SOUP—TOMATO, canned—and the girls giggled. Paula didn't so much as bother glaring at him. Grilled cheese sandwiches and soup made for the laziest dinner she could remember serving in a long time, but when she got home and realized she hadn't stopped for groceries, she thought to herself, *Fuck it, they won't even notice.* Rigby would have bitched about it, but he wasn't here, was he?

Isolde started on the second half of her sandwich, having taken only two bites out of the first, and Fiona scowled. "Mom, she's doing it again."

"I don't care," Paula said. The girls both got along fine with their brother, but they worked hard to drive each other crazy, and they knew one another's weak points intimately.

"I'm going to eat both halves," Isolde said. "Why do you care what order I do it in?"

"That's it, I'm done." Fiona stood, her dinner unfinished. She seemed to be waiting for Paula to order her to sit back down, and it took a good twenty seconds before she took her plate to the kitchen counter. Then she started eating her sandwich again, over the sink. Her sister continued to chew, managing to smirk at the same time.

"Can I have a hundred dollars?" Danny asked.

"What for?"

"I want to see Lil Bohunk at Hollywood Forever in two weeks."

"Who?"

"Lil Bohunk. He's a rapper."

"Is he dead?"

"I wouldn't be paying a hundred dollars to see him if he was dead, Mom."

"I thought Hollywood Forever was a cemetery."

"They also have concerts," he said with such forbearance that she decided to give him the hundred. Why not? A hundred dollars more or less wasn't going to save them from ruin.

"How are you getting down there?"

"Jonah's driving."

"I don't know how I feel about you riding with Jonah."

"If I had my own car, like literally every single one of my friends—"

She held up her hand. "All right, we'll talk about this another time. You can have the hundred."

AFTER DINNER, SHE SAT down and figured out what her income was likely to be over the next three months if every single one of her listings sold for the asking price and every single one of her clients bought a house for more or less what they'd decided they could afford. It was a wildly optimistic scenario, even childishly so. Then she figured out what they owed and made a similarly optimistic stab at how long the bank was likely to let the mortgage situation slide. The house was so far underwater there wasn't any point in putting it on the market and downsizing.

She saw no way around losing it. They had six months, max. Foreclosure was bad news for anybody, but for a realtor at her level, it could be a career-ender. She didn't know what had really happened with Rigby and Haskill's supposedly stolen money, though she suspected the whole thing existed as a fantasy in her husband's mind, but his reassurances that he had a follow-up plan didn't comfort her. Time, maybe, to start thinking seriously about talking to a divorce lawyer and saving whatever assets could still be saved.

CHAPTER NINE

WHEN THE OLD MAN yelled down the staircase instead of using the intercom, she continued sipping her coffee, filled in another answer in the crossword—seventeen across, *zygomatic*—and waited for him to yell again. When it came, considerably louder and higher in pitch this time, in a tone that conveyed exaggerated, undue wrath and anguish, she leaned back in her chair and glanced at the clock on the stove. Eight forty-nine. She hit the intercom button.

"Mr. Haskill? Did I hear you yelling?"

Another incoherent yell came from upstairs and she hit the button again. "Mr. Haskill? Was that you?"

The intercom crackled, followed by his weary voice. "I need you, Nina. Please get up here immediately."

She mounted the staircase, carrying his morning meds and cold breakfast on a tray. Entering the bedroom, she moved to the window and opened the drapes. He was sitting up, arms folded across his chest. "I don't know why you can't hear me when I yell. Before we put in that damned intercom you heard me just fine, it seems to me."

"Mr. Haskill, that's not true. I usually didn't hear you until the third or fourth time. If it's an emergency, I don't want to have to rely on my ears or your croaky old voice." She set the tray down on his night table and crossed her arms. "Now, what's the matter, Mr. Haskill?"

"Why won't you call me Glenn? My last assistant called me Glenn."

"This isn't Hollywood, Mr. Haskill, this is Santa Barbara. I don't address my employers that way."

"It makes it awkward for me to call you Nina, and I don't want to call you Miss Nordmann."

"It'd be Ms. Nordmann. And you calling me by my first name doesn't bother me at all. Anything else?"

"My lawyer's coming at noon. Make sure there's a lunch ready, please. Red meat. He says he doesn't eat it, but if you set a steak in front of him, he sure will."

"That's already on my calendar. That all?"

"Did you answer that email from the young fellow wanted to interview me about *Midnight Squad?*"

"I will as soon as you tell me what to say to him."

"I'll think about it."

"All right. I'm going to get groceries in half an hour, if you think of anything special you want, buzz me."

"I'll holler."

"Use the intercom or I'll ignore you."

AN HOUR LATER AT the supermarket, standing next to the prepackaged beef case, she spotted an oddly familiar-looking woman wearing sunglasses, eyes behind them darting this way and that as though scanning for some nearby deadly danger. An elderly and very slow-moving couple pushed their cart past her, and the husband glanced innocently in her direction. The woman shot her gaze up to the ceiling with an exaggeratedly put-upon air, though the old man seemed to Nina to be glancing at the tri-tip special at the end of the cooler and not at the woman. That was when it clicked; she was an actress, one whose closest brush with fame had come in the early nineties. The woman's name escaped her at the

moment, but she'd nearly been big once. This naked longing for recognition made Nina's teeth itch. As she leaned
into the meat case to grab her filets, she glanced back at the
actress and said, "Funny how time slips away." She put them
into her basket and headed for checkout.

"Hey, Nina," the checker said. "Steak for dinner, huh."

"Lunch."

"You're going to kill that old man."

"He's too old for this to make any difference. Might as
well get him started smoking again. Or get him some crystal
meth, see how he likes that."

FOR THE MOST PART, she tolerated the leering ways of
Haskill's elderly male friends, relics as they were of a very
different generation from her own. Rigby was different. For
one thing, he was only in his forties and avoided making
dirty comments in her presence. But there was something
about his patronizing way of asking her opinion on business matters in which she had no interest or involvement,
about his asking after her distant family that she found as
off-putting as the ordinary, blatant lechery of the old men.

Today he was exuberantly praising her cooking and
wondering whether she'd ever thought about returning to
school.

"One MFA's useless enough."

Haskill held up a finger for silence as he finished chewing
a large bite of his meat. When he finished, he wiped his
lips, smacking. "Nina's a very intelligent young woman. She
could go back and do anything she wants, intellectually
speaking. I want to discuss putting a provision for her future
education into the will, Rigby."

She shrugged. "Thanks, Mr. Haskill, but I'm not going
back."

"Nonsense, young lady. I know a lack of funds is the only thing keeping you from a doctorate."

This wasn't the case at all, and she didn't believe for an instant that the old man and Rigby were planning to provide her with anything whatsoever. She'd never once mentioned a desire to go back to grad school, which she'd hated the first time around anyway.

When they were finished eating, she collected the plates and stacked them in the sink. When she got back to the table, they were deep in conversation. "Either of you want coffee?"

"Not I," Haskill said. "Sit down, you'll find this interesting. It's about art."

Since discovering that her background was in art history, he'd been trying to get her interested in his ghastly art collection, awful pictures of hard-bitten cowboys and sad, noble Indians by fourth-tier Remington and Russell imitators. There were some badly modeled bronzes, too, all purchased from the same gallery in New Mexico. She pulled out her phone and started browsing, knowing it drove the old man crazy but that he wouldn't say anything about it.

But Haskill and Rigby were intently discussing the crappy artwork, and she zoned out quickly, absorbed in a string of dog pictures her sister had posted. Of late, she'd been mulling over a return to the East Coast and what she considered civilization. California had never suited her very well, and now she found herself a so-called personal assistant, which amounted to a cross between a secretary and a live-in nurse.

Wait. She looked up from a shot of a sprightly dachshund-Chihuahua mix at the sound of a name and started listening, and there it was again: Kushik. The only decent picture in the house, the only one worth money.

"There's a really first-rate art collection there and I'd like to add to it," Haskill said.

Rigby nodded, jotting some figures down on a legal pad. "I think it's worth, say, ten grand, that'll be a nice deduction for the estate, and I'm sure Jerry'd rather have that than the picture."

"I'm sorry, what about the Kushik? You're giving it away?"

"Once I've croaked, or maybe before," Haskill said. "I know it's the only thing in the collection you like. I'm giving it to my old school. Rigby knows why."

"I do," he said, looking like he'd rather not hear it again.

"Why?" she said.

"One day in 1937 the headmaster called me in and lectured the hell out of me. Some little snitch spotted me smoking behind the main building." Nina raised an eyebrow. "Okay, I knew that was against the rules. But the old bastard proceeded to pull out my file and went through it class by class, year by year and read me every nasty comment every teacher'd made. Boy, they all had it out for little Glenn. And my parents were shelling out a pretty penny to send me there, you'd think they'd have a little more respect. Anyway, the headmaster, Mr. Ebbing, he told me right to my face and told me I wasn't ever going to amount to anything."

"And here you are," she said.

"And here I am, donating a picture to the school that's worth somewhere north of ten grand."

Resisting the temptation to set them straight about the painting's value, she favored him with a tiny simulacrum of a smile. Half-listening to the conversation about the disposition of the rest of the artwork she studied Rigby's face carefully, trying to determine whether he was already working on a con or, if he wasn't, how receptive he'd be to signing on for one, because she knew for a fact that Haskill was ripe for a posthumous grift. She had a sense that there wasn't much Rigby wouldn't be up for, regardless of his client's best interests.

WHEN SHE WAS FINISHED with the dishes she detected a hint of a familiar, foul odor, and she followed it to the living room, where she found Rigby seated across the room from her employer, cigar in hand. He pointed at the old man.

"He made me do it, Nina, I swear."

"I just wanted the smell," Haskill said.

"You've got me mistaken for a nurse," she said.

"This is my house." The old man's lower lip jutted out, purple and wet. "I just wanted the smell."

Rigby, meanwhile, smirked like a naughty eight-year-old, and she understood that she was ruining their fun. Her predecessor had taken this part of her job seriously, the part where she was supposed to enforce doctor's orders, the part where she was the killjoy female authority figure.

All right, why not? She crossed over to Rigby, took the cigar from his hand and left the room. Once the door shut behind her she heard them giggling like little boys. She extinguished the cigar in the kitchen sink with a stinking hiss, then returned to the living room and interrupted Rigby in mid-sentence. "You're supposed to be his friend and counsel. Better start acting like it."

"I made him do it, Nina," Haskill said.

"You be quiet. I'll deal with you later."

"Glenn, she's absolutely right, I should have turned you down. Nina, do you forgive me?"

She sat down in a stiff, under-upholstered wing chair that was the epitome of the late Evvie Haskill's taste in furnishings: elegant, expensive and uncomfortable. "Just watch it from now on," she said, trying hard to invest the phrase with meaning. The two men sat in silence for twenty seconds, and she leaned forward. "Well, go on, don't stop talking on my account."

Rigby grinned, and it made him look rabid. "Glenn was in the middle of a dirty story when you caught me smoking."

"I've heard worse, I promise."

Haskill smirked. "Have you ever heard of a thing called the casting couch?"

"Sure."

He sat up a little straighter and with his palm smoothed the little patch of white hair on the side of his head. "The one in my office saw a lot of action in my day."

It took her a second to understand that he was actually proud of it. "So basically actresses would let you have sex with them to get into TV shows?"

"Exactly!" He was as animated as she'd seen him, his long, thin, yellow teeth bared in nostalgic glee. "If you saw a pretty girl on one of my shows so much as answering a telephone, you could bet your bottom dollar I'd made her first."

"Literally on the couch?"

"As a matter of fact yes, although for a while I had an apartment off of Larchmont, few blocks from the Desilu lot when we were doing *Colonel Tundra*. Had to give that up when Evvie found out about it."

"So she knew about some of it?" Rigby said. He sounded envious.

"She didn't want to know. She was good at not seeing things. And she wasn't so innocent herself. When I first met her, she was running after Lon Chaney, Jr."

"The Wolf Man?" Rigby said.

"She liked that deep, rich voice of his. She'd find out where he was working—usually Poverty Row, he was halfway on the skids by then—and she'd wait outside the studio gates."

"What would she have done if she'd caught him?"

"Fucked him, I guess. She claimed she never succeeded."

"That didn't give you pause, a woman telling you she was stalking another man?" Nina asked.

"Oh, they didn't call it stalking back then. I could tell she was crazy, if that's what you mean. I liked that. Plus, don't forget, at that age she was a very beautiful girl with big tits and a nice caboose, and I wasn't thinking 'hey, maybe I'll marry her.' I just wanted to top her. She was so hard to get I asked her to marry me just to get to third base, and what do you know, she said yes, and it turned out okay for fifty-plus years."

There were times when Glenn Haskill repulsed her, and there were times when she found him almost endearing.

CHAPTER TEN

BILLY HAD BEEN IN the C store for ten minutes without buying anything or even picking something up as though considering its purchase, and the clerk was giving him the stink eye. He looked like a shoplifter, he knew, because he'd been caught all seven times he'd tried it, even though every single time he'd been sure he had the secret down. He'd managed to avoid conviction on six of those, and had skated with a year's probation on the seventh for a pack of Bubblicious Lightning Lemonade with LeBron James's face on the package. It was funny thinking about that now, because it would be weeks at the very least before he'd be able to chew gum.

"You need help finding whatever it is you're looking for?" the clerk asked in a deep, slow monotone from behind the register. He was well over six feet tall with a shiny gray face, and when he leaned over the counter he was an imposing sight, a little scary, even, Billy thought.

"Nah, I'm good," he said as best he could with his jaw wired shut. The fact was he was high enough on Vicodin the emergency room docs had given him that he couldn't remember what he'd gone out looking for.

"What's the matter with your voice?"

"What's the matter with yours," he tried to say, but he knew it had come out as gibberish.

"Dude, are you high right now?"

"Nuh-uh," he managed, and to illustrate he opened his lips wide to show the scaffolding in his mouth.

"Wow, sorry, man, that fucking sucks. Hey, are you Magda's boyfriend?"

That stopped him for a moment. This guy knew Magda? He nodded.

"Seen you on the street with her a time or two. I used to take my cat there when I was in Ojai."

Billy nodded.

"I was surprised to see her in Moorpark. Tell her Big Lester's still got that three-legged Siamese, would you?"

He nodded and picked a canned strawberry kiwi smoothie from the refrigerator case. He didn't want to listen to this creep talk about Magda. He still had thirty-two bucks and change left over from the trip to Needles, so he bought a couple of five-dollar bingo scratchers as well.

Twenty minutes later, he was sitting at Magda's kitchen table drinking the smoothie through a kid's bendy straw and grooving on the Vicodin—he'd taken a second, because he really fucking hurt and also because he liked the way it felt— and wondering whether he'd won or not on the scratchers. He'd never played bingo before, and he couldn't make heads or tails of the explanation on the back of the card. It had taken him a good half an hour to get done scratching all the numbers and marking the appropriate boxes, and he'd found it fairly diverting, though without the opioids he would have been frustrated to the point of scratching his own eyes out. The Mighty Morphin Power Rangers were on the TV with the sound off, and the set was old and broken, so the colors weren't right, but that was okay.

After the question of the scratchers, his attention was

mostly on a dope-addled plan to get Magda to let him move in with her, because his old place on Ventura Avenue wasn't safe anymore, not with that nutty lawyer knowing where it was and how thin the door was and shit. Plus, what was the use of paying two rents?

Downstairs a car honked, the sound followed by that of a collision, and he rose slowly and made his uncertain way to the window. A Buick had just T-boned a gardener's pickup in the middle of the intersection, pretty much demolishing the bed right behind the cab. The Buick driver stepped out, old and white, and addressed the truck driver, middle-aged and Chicano. The old man was pointing and screaming as if he weren't the one who'd broadsided the other guy and the truck driver just stood there looking at the contorted metal and shaking his head. Billy unlatched the window and raised it to listen, and he had a good laugh until the cops got there. Out of instinct and long habit, he pulled his head back inside and lowered the sash, but he kept watching and got another laugh when the old man got the ticket, still yelling and pointing at the truck driver.

He laid down for a while on Magda's couch, and his brain filled with a happy memory of doing it indoors with her for the first time on that very couch back when she still lived in Ojai down the street from her nasty old hippie mother. Its upholstery was frayed and its stuffing lumpy, but he felt as comfortable there at that moment as he ever had in any bed or beanbag chair. Maybe it was the Vicodin. He could give up crank for this stuff, he thought, but he was afraid of getting addicted. Maybe he could use the two to take the edge off each other, though.

He scratched at a loose section of fabric, took hold of a little thread and twisted it around until it unraveled itself and got straight. He was going to get Magda a new couch someday. A nice one with leather instead of cloth, but they'd keep this one for old times' sake. He started thinking again about the five grand the psycho lawyer owed him. It was hard having something like that dangling in front of you and then having it snatched away, like teasing a cat with a piece of meat you don't really intend to let him have.

He thought about his cats. They were probably worried about whether he was okay or not. Poor kitties. He got sad thinking about them, wondering who'd feed them.

He was back at the table, working on the smoothie when Magda got home and slammed the door.

"Have you seriously been sitting there at that table since I went to work this morning?"

He shook his head and explained to the best of his ability that he'd been down to the convenience store and also to the window and on the couch, too.

"And watching kiddie TV. Nice and productive."

"I got a broken jaw," he said as best he could.

"I know, but this is why I don't want you hanging here when I'm gone. You make yourself too much at home. If you had a job it'd keep you busy, at least."

"Sorry," he said, feeling bad about his sibilant "s."

She drew up behind him and embraced him. "I'm sorry, baby. I had a rough day. That Dr. Perkins is a real sack of shit. I'm halfway ready to bail on that job."

This sent a shiver of panic through him. He'd never had a girlfriend with a steady job before, and that was a large part of the attraction here. Not so much the fact that she had disposable income—she didn't spend it on him, anyway—but the idea that she was a productive member of society. If she was willing to pair off with him, maybe that meant he had a shot of getting there someday himself.

Then something amazing happened, at least by his

standards. He remembered the message! He'd walked home stewing about the C store clerk's mentioning Magda, and when he got inside he'd written it down, imagining that if he didn't deliver it the man might use the fact against him somehow.

"Hey, I got something to tell you about the guy in the store." He looked down at his loopier-than-usual scrawl. "Wesley still has the three-headed Chinese."

"Jesus, Billy, how fucking high are you, anyway?" She started rolling a joint. "Today, Dr. Ma was examining this old black lab with arthritic knees and Perkins came over and told her right in front of a client how her diagnosis was wrong, which it wasn't, because she's a way better vet than Perkins ever was. I think he's drinking over lunchtime. And he leers at women clients, especially the young ones."

Billy nodded and made a sympathetic sound of encouragement.

"So did you see that crash downstairs? Looks like a pretty good one."

His face brightened and he nodded.

She lit up and took a long drag, after which Billy reached for the joint. She pulled it out of his reach. "Nuh-uh, not while you're on the pain meds." The look on his face must have been even sadder than he felt, because she immediately relented and handed it to him.

He took a hit and handed it back to her and tried to explain how discombobulated he was over the whole business of the five thousand dollars. She got up and once again embraced him from behind. "Poor, sweet baby," she murmured, blowing smoke into his ear.

Between the mandibular gear and the opioids, he had a hard time getting started, but he managed to make his case to Magda that he wasn't safe in his old apartment, but instead of coming to his intended conclusion that the only answer was to allow him to move in with her, her instinct was to confront the problem head-on.

"I hate seeing what he did to you. We can't just let that asshole beat you up and steal your money."

He shrugged and said, or tried to say, "What else I got?"

"How about we put a scare into him, what do you say?"

CHAPTER ELEVEN

RIGBY WAS ALMOST BACK to Ventura when he got the text. Steering with his left hand he held the phone in his right.

CALL ME THIS AFTERNOON

He pressed the phone against the soft center of the steering wheel and typed.

WHOS THIS

A minute later:

NINA

Then:

DON'T TELL MR HASKILL CONFIDENTIAL BUSINESS BET U AND ME

Huh. He thumbed in:

WILL DO

Just then a CHP cruiser pulled up next to him and he let the phone drop to the floor. Fucking Chippies, always showing up at the exact wrong moment. The cops didn't look over at him, though, and the cruiser sped up and pulled back into the right-hand lane a couple of car lengths ahead of him.

He didn't know whether or not he hoped this was a come-on. There was a peculiar coldness to Nina's affect that intimated something not too far from psychosis, a chilly lack of affect that was arousing and off-putting at the same time;

he wondered if she had dominant tendencies. You never knew with the quiet, mousy type, sometimes they were freaks in the sack. That might be fun sometime, having a lady treat him like dirt, smack him around a little bit, maybe. Was that what had old Glenn eating out of her hand like that? He'd never seen him defer to anyone the way he did to Nina.

If she wanted to hook up, he was good with that, though he suspected it might get even more complicated than he liked things to get. Best to assume it was business.

At his feet the phone buzzed again. He knew it was better to wait until he could pull over, but he had a good idea of where it sat in relation to his foot. Gently he eased off of the gas and raised his left foot, and with his right hand he reached between his legs, eyes still on the road, to fish around on the floor. He felt nothing but the carpet and in frustration he shot his gaze downward, and the instant he spotted the phone he raised his eyes to the road in time to see the front end of the Escalade about to collide with the rear end of the CHP cruiser.

He swerved off onto the shoulder with a terrified "Fuck!" After rolling a few crunchy feet on the gravel, he stopped and turned the engine off, and as the cruiser put on its lights and pulled over ahead of him, then went into reverse, he ran through his meager options. Then, despite the considerable risk to his person that this action entailed, he opened the door of the car and jumped out, waving his arms frantically at the open door, as though trying to shoo something from the Escalade's interior.

"Put your fucking hands on top of your head!" There were two officers standing outside the cruiser, one of them pointing his service revolver at Rigby, the other next to the passenger door on the radio.

He put both hands on his head. "Sorry," he yelled. "There was a bee in the car, it landed on my hand and I panicked."

"Keep your hands on your head."

Both officers approached gingerly, and the second officer put on a pair of latex gloves. "Is there anything in your pocket that's going to stick me or otherwise cause me harm?"

"No, Officer. Wallet's in my right-hand front pocket."

The officer removed the wallet and examined his license. "Mr. Rigby, do you know why I approached you with my weapon drawn?"

"Yes sir, Officer, sorry, I know I shouldn't have gotten out. But I'm allergic to bees."

"You could have easily been shot to death."

"I understand, I'm sorry. But a bee sting could have been fatal, too."

The officer with his gun drawn replaced it in its holster, his face puffy and tired. "You sure you weren't texting?"

"Never, Officer. I have a son of driving age, and I try real hard to be a good example to him. As a driver."

"You can put your hands down," the second cop said. He was younger than his partner, and had a deep, nasty scar cutting across his nose that Rigby wished he could ask about. He handed the wallet back. "You carry an EpiPen in your glove box? That'd be a real good idea."

"I do in my own car, today I'm driving my wife's. Probably I ought to get one for it, too."

"Do that, Mr. Rigby. And please remember, next time you exit your vehicle during a traffic stop you might not survive the experience."

"Thanks, officers. I appreciate your understanding."

HE GOT BACK INTO the car, exhilarated by his skills as a liar. He felt as if his soul were glowing from within his chest.

He picked up the phone. The text wasn't from Nina, but an unidentified 805 number. It read, GIVE ME MY MONEY OR U BEST WATCH OUT U MIGHT GET WACKD + MY DOCTR BILLS 2

He tossed the phone onto the seat next to him and pulled back onto the 101, favoring the Chippies with a curt wave as he passed the parked cruiser and wondering how Billy Knox managed to get his real cell number.

AT SIX-THIRTY, HE WAS waiting for Nina at the bar of the Sportsman downtown. He suggested it as a meeting place because it was dark and evocative of secret assignations and because if it did turn out she was interested in something down-low and dirty, the crowd there didn't know his wife. On the mirror behind the bar were etched two gleeful cowgirls brandishing six-shooters, wearing skimpy vests but otherwise topless. Judging by their hairstyles, Rigby guessed that they'd been etched in the glass sometime in the 1940s; how the hell had they gotten away with such a thing back then?

Nina arrived, took a cursory look at her surroundings and shook her head. "We need to get a booth."

He signaled the hostess and she directed them to a red Naugahyde booth, above which hung an obscenely large, spidery king crab, mounted and framed. "So am I to understand you have some sort of legal problem you'd like help with?"

"Nothing like that. It's not a problem, even. More of an opportunity."

"I like opportunities."

"So the painting you were talking about giving away to Mr. Haskill's school."

"The Russian one."

"The Kushik. He thinks it's worth ten grand, I don't know

where you guys came up with a figure like that. You didn't get a proper appraisal."

It was a statement of fact, not a question. The look of disdain was the first discernible expression that had crossed her face since she sat down, and knowing her dislike for Haskill's art collection he tried appealing to her snobbery. "It's not the fucking Norton Simon in there, Nina."

She bent her swizzle stick. "So? Where'd you come up with ten grand on the Kushik?"

"I don't know, I think I looked up an old auction record at the library. You want recent auction records online, you have to pay."

She leaned forward and flicked a few drops of her whiskey sour at his face. He couldn't tell if the gesture was flirtatious, contemptuous or accidental. "I'm just telling you this because I don't want the estate to lose a whole lot of money. That painting's worth seven figures, easy."

He felt his heartbeat quicken, even though he was sure this was bogus. "That would be a major increase," he said with as little inflection as he could manage.

"He was Russian. The last fifteen, twenty years, these rich Russians have been buying up all the exiles' works. Kushik was one of the best."

"Huh." He didn't care for the picture much more than the rest of Glenn's paintings, but then he didn't like a lot of things that society had decided were worth something.

"Trust me on this. My thesis advisor was a Russian specialist, and I know more about this stuff than I want to. That picture's worth more than the house is."

"So it'd be a mistake to hand the school the picture, is what you're suggesting?"

"If he's doing it for spite, yeah."

"It's a lot to chew on."

"There's something else. I'm assuming it's never been authenticated, right? Appraised by anyone who knew the work?"

"Oh, it's real, all right. Evvie was great pals with Kushik's widow, the picture was a birthday present."

"I know it's real just looking. Listen, though. What if the school was given a fake? It probably wouldn't find out for years, until they did an appraisal of their collection. Even if they did it right away, after Mr. Haskill's death, it'd just look like he got cheated by some dealer."

"Uh-huh." He had a feeling he knew what she was going to propose, but he wanted her to be the first to say it.

"Meanwhile, there'd be an authentic Kushik for the Russian market."

Goddamn it, she was crookeder than he was. "I like the way you think. Now let me ask you, where would one procure, if one were so inclined, a fake Kushik?"

"That's the big question, isn't it?"

THAT NIGHT AT TEN, he parked around the corner from Billy Knox's miserable little crib and climbed the stairs to the third floor. He had a baseball cap pulled low in front in case any of the neighbors were watching, but this was the sort of building where no one saw much of anything no matter what happened. He rapped on Billy's door.

In his jacket pocket he carried a filleting knife. It would have made a shitty murder weapon, but he guessed it was enough to frighten the likes of Billy, and anyway he didn't intend to actually harm the little fucker. In his shirt pocket was a hundred-dollar bill, intended as a consolation prize. Worst-case scenario, he'd re-break Billy's jaw, or maybe his arms.

He knocked again, waited two minutes, then tried the

handle. It was unlocked, and inside the mess and the stench were considerably worse than before, a mixture of days-old garbage and shit. A pair of cats slipped out between his feet as he stood there with the door open, howling as they descended the staircase. He turned on the light switch next to the door and saw that the furniture was all gone, except for a stripped-bare, piss-stained mattress on the dingy carpet. The cats' litter box was overflowing with turds, the food and water bowls empty. Fucking Billy, what kind of sicko would abandon his cats and take everything else? The same kind of dumb fuck who'd give away a big batch of coke, he guessed.

At the bottom of the stairs he found the cats, sniffing at the jamb. He opened the door and they shot out into the night. Probably they were better off in the wild than they'd been with Billy Knox. He hoped so, anyway.

CHAPTER TWELVE

HE WAS STACKING WOMEN'S sweaters on a low circular table when she walked into the pro shop and started talking to Barton. "Hey, Paula," he called to her, and she returned an ostentatiously casual wave.

"Hi, Keith," she said, her perfectly arched left eyebrow lifted. Her face was slightly asymmetrical to begin with, something you didn't notice until you'd been concentrating on it for a long time. When she turned her full attention to Barton he felt his abdominal muscles tighten.

He continued to arrange the table, pastels of varying shades going more or less according to the color wheel as he remembered it—was there a particular order, warm to cool or vice versa?—and pretending not to listen to the conversation between Paula and Barton. She was looking for a windbreaker for her husband's birthday.

"He doesn't play golf, does he, Mrs. Rigby?"

"No, but he wears windbreakers and likes the club logo. Or he likes to let people know he's a member."

Buying a gift for her husband there at the pro shop? It was some kind of mind game, he knew that much, but her skill level was way beyond his. Was she trying to make him jealous or trying to be funny? Jesus. Was there something weird about the way she'd waved? About her voice, addressing him? Was there an appreciable sex vibe between them? He was certain there was; the question was, could Barton read it? If he were caught having an affair with a member, it would mean his job, and though they got along all right as coworkers, it was a competitive workplace, and he knew Barton would sell him out without compunction.

He'd never thought of himself as the kind of guy who'd knock boots with a married lady. But the way she'd started coming on to him, slowly at first, flirting during lessons—nothing unusual about that, as long as you didn't act on it—then getting more and more direct, finally flat out telling him that, as far as she was concerned, it was going to happen. He wasn't in love with her, he didn't think. The notion of her leaving her husband to come live with him had never occurred to him, in fact. But he thought about her all the time, about how she looked clothed and unclothed, about the things she said to him during, before and after, about what she might be doing at a given time of day, about what she did with her husband. About whether she did the same things with Rigby she did with him.

The problem was, the thing was making him a nervous wreck. It was starting to affect his game, and lately giving lessons he found himself looking at some of his other flirtatious lady students and asking himself whether he should try to take things a step further. He knew that was the way a lot of pros got burned and ended up working in call centers or drive-throughs. Maybe it was time to break it off, start taking Mo seriously and look to the future.

But while Barton's back was turned toward the rack, Paula favored him with a glance so sultry and playful that he felt his face start to burn and had to turn away, pretending to realign a display of titanium drivers.

"What's his size?" Barton asked.

"You've seen him, right? He's a bodybuilder, so probably extra large."

And here was another of Paula's games, pointing out Rigby's physical prowess and the prospect of severe physical damage if he ever found out someone was putting the meat to his missus, as she charmingly put it. He'd met Rigby three times and had found him to be glib but agreeable on each occasion, more so the more alcohol he'd consumed, but he had no trouble imagining him in a violent rage and had no doubt that he was capable of doing serious damage if provoked.

Then Mo walked in wearing her waitress uniform, wholesome, strawberry-blond, pretty Mo, and he felt his blood pressure rising in panic. "Hey Keith, you got lunch coming up? I got cut and I'm going to Bert's downtown. Join me?"

She navigated the maze of displays and grabbed him by the biceps and kissed him. Panicking, he barely kissed her in return.

"Barton, look at Keith," Paula said in a tone of rich amusement, with the merest sardonic hint of a smile on that lovely mouth. "He's blushing."

"DID YOU SENSE KIND of a weird vibe between Barton and that lady?" Mo said between bites of an enormous, greasy BLT.

"How do you mean?"

"There was just something sexy about her talking to him."

"Not in a million years. He'd be fired."

"I didn't mean anything was actually going on. But she was flirting."

"She's not the type." He knew it was ridiculous to be offended by the insinuation, but he felt a duty to defend her. "She's a married mother of three."

Mo snorted. "Right, and that kind never gets in any trouble."

"It's just, she's a nice lady."

Mo nodded and took a long swig of her iced tea. "So we're invited to Big Bear next weekend? My friend Amy and her husband are renting a big cabin, and there's a room for us if we want. Chloe's going and some other people I don't know."

He took a bite of his club sandwich and watched the pedestrians on Main, trying to think of an answer. "Actually, I can't."

"You're off work."

"I took on some private lessons. You could go without me."

"The cabin isn't the point. I thought we were spending the weekend together."

"Sorry."

"Jesus, Keith." She slapped the table with both hands, then flipped them, holding them palms up, fingers splayed. "You told me you were off next weekend. That's why I took it off."

"Sorry."

She leaned back and crossed her arms. "You don't take me very seriously."

That was true, but he wasn't convinced it always would be. If there were only a way to keep her on the hook until he was ready to be finished with Paula. "Sorry."

She pushed the plate away from her.

"Look, you didn't say anything about going to Mammoth."

"Big Bear. It's Big Bear."

"All right, you didn't say anything about taking a trip."

"No, but we talked about doing something. I thought we'd have a weekend together without work."

"Sorry."

"If you say you're sorry one more time, I'm going to get really pissed."

He wanted to tell her how pretty she was, mad like this, but it so happened that Paula had, only two weeks before, explained to him that this particular male de-escalation strategy was a good way to get kneed in the ball sack. "Maybe I should get back to work," he said, and he reached for the check.

She was looking at her empty iced tea glass. "I just want you to know that I turned down an invitation to Palm Springs next month with your friend Barton."

"He's not my friend."

"And that doesn't piss you off? That he asked?"

"I guess it does."

"You guess?"

"Well, you said no, didn't you? You can't blame him for trying."

"What's that mean?"

"It means look at you, you're beautiful and smart. And I probably don't deserve you."

She studied him as though trying to gauge his sincerity. He was self-aware enough to know that most people underestimated his intelligence and therefore his guile-fulness. "Probably not," she said, but she was smiling when she said it.

THAT NIGHT, HE ATE a Trader Joe's burrito while he watched an episode of *The Simpsons*. This was a scenario he repeated approximately three hundred times a year, and as soon as the episode ended, he rinsed his dish in the sink and headed out the door.

On the sidewalk out front his landlady stood in a ratty pink housedress, spraying the bougainvilleas with a black garden hose, her big pale feet in flip-flops. "Disposal working all right now?"

"Working fine, Lorna."

"Good. I want my tenants happy."

It had taken three weeks of complaints before she'd finally sent over a handyman, but Keith cut her a fair amount of slack. The rent was cheap, and most of the time she was a nice old lady.

He stuck to the north side of Thompson Avenue until he was within sight of the bar. When he reached the comic book store, he lingered for a minute, looking through the window, then jogged across the street and walked inside.

The Town Crier was quiet even by the standards of a Tuesday in May, the lovely evening outside and the smell of flowers and the ocean keeping people away from dark, stinky indoor spaces. A quartet of college boys played pool without skill or enthusiasm, a few fossilized regulars sat muttering into their drinks and tall, gregarious Brenda was working the sticks.

She pulled him a draft without asking and placed it on the damp bar in front of him. "Hey, Keith. So guess what I talked to my lawyer about today? Restraining order."

"Jesus. Really?"

"No fooling. Gary comes over last night about two-thirty, right after I got home, tries to put his old key in the door, starts pounding on it and yelling when it doesn't work. Two years since the divorce was official, and he's surprised I changed the locks. He starts yelling, 'You cunt, let me in my house,' and I said, 'It's not your house anymore, and if you call me a cunt one more time, I'll call the cops and we'll see what your probation officer has to say about that.' So he left. Not before waking the kids, both of whom had school in the morning."

"What's the lawyer say about the restraining order?"

"Says it's tricky because if I file one and word gets back to his P.O., he's back in jail, which is fine with me, but I worry about the kids getting a little older and knowing their dad's in prison. On the other hand, if I don't, he's liable to kill me sometime."

He liked the scenario of the ex going back to prison but kept his counsel, as this was the kind of advice that could come back and bite you in the ass if a couple reconciled and confidences were shared. "Well, be careful. What's Mickey have to say about it?"

She snorted. "Mickey's scared shitless, that big fat pussy. He's twice as big as Gary, but he said he couldn't come over tonight because his dog's sick. I'm about ready to drop that asshole, maybe hook up with somebody with a little more brass in their balls. Or maybe I should hold out for some-body with a job, maybe I could quit one or two of mine."

"You still waiting tables at the Old Formosa?"

"Nope, they had me down to two shifts so I said see ya. That place is a magnet for cheapskates anyway, tips barely covered the sitter, nights when my mom couldn't do it. I got two shifts a week at Pottery Shack."

She sniffled, ran her finger under her dripping nose, then rubbed at her bloodshot red eye with the same finger. "Damn, my eye's killing me tonight."

"Quit rubbing it."

"It itches."

"You're going to get a sty if you don't cut that out."

"Yeah, all right, Doc." She sighed, looking at the boys at the pool table. "Think I should have carded them? I've seen two or three of them in here before."

"Not for me to say."

"The tall skinny one's a good tipper. I think he likes me."

"Wouldn't surprise me." Lots of guys liked Brenda. "Maybe you should give the whole cougar business a shot."

The front door opened and a wary Bobby Theele peered in, wearing his ratty old winter coat despite the season, checking to see who was behind the bar. Seeing Brenda, he cautiously proceeded, walking the slow, delicate minuet of a drunk trying to look sober. This was a giveaway, because sober or only slightly wasted Bobby was an inveterate stumbler.

"Nope," Brenda said.

Bobby reached the bar and took a stool. "Come on, Bren. I'm fine." He leaned down so close to the bar that his tangled gray beard almost touched it, and Keith could smell the stale sauce on his breath three stools away. Bobby was the owner, and when he got too drunk to be served anywhere else he showed up at his own place; this would be his fourth or fifth stop of the night.

"Promised your wife I wouldn't when you got like this. I'll call you a cab if you want."

"Screw you, you rotten bitch." He looked like a cornered, elderly, injured wolf, yellow teeth bared and pure hate in his eyes. "I own this shithole and I'll fire you on the spot."

"Now, Bobby, no you won't, Constance won't let you. And on paper, she's as much the owner as you," she said, no offense taken. "I'll give you one shot, and then you go home in a taxi."

He leaned back, arms folded across his chest and a defiant glare on his face. "Fuck you." His bulbous eyes shone in the reflected light of an ancient Hamm's beer ad, a slow-rolling panorama of glistening river and faded mountain. The big rectangular stained-glass light fixture above the pool table also pushed Hamm's. When was the last time that particular beer was available here or anywhere, Keith wondered as Brenda poured Bobby a shot of Old Grand-Dad.

Bobby stared at it, arms still folded. "Gimme a chaser and it's a deal."

She opened him a Bud Light and set it on the bar in front of him, then picked up the house phone to call the cab company.

"Thank you, Brenda," he said quietly, dignity compromised but intact. Once he'd swallowed the shot and taken a healthy swig of the beer, the nature of his drunkenness transformed. He sat up straight and addressed Keith, his diction slightly clearer than before, one bushy, gray eyebrow arched in amusement.

"Well, if it isn't Arnie Palmer himself, relaxing after a hard day instructing the haute bourgeoisie of Ventura County in the arcane secrets of the links."

"Oat what? Some kind of breakfast cereal, Bobby?"

He squinted at Keith and pointed at his nose. "Don't be smart. Rumors of war afoot, my lad. Mind they don't draft you."

"There isn't a draft anymore," Keith pointed out, "and I'm thirty-four, anyway."

"Cannon fodder, once they run out of young ones. You better get yourself some kind of injury. Once they raise the draft age, a fine athlete like you'd be on the way to the front lines to fight the Hun."

"I don't think it's Germany we're fighting anymore."

Bobby swatted at an imaginary housefly in front of his nose. "The dusky Christ-deniers, then. Point is, you ought to get yourself an injury. Lose a toe, say."

"That'd play hell with my backswing. My sense of balance is my livelihood."

The front door opened once again, and Bobby took a sad look in that direction, expecting the grim figure of the cabbie, but in his stead was Paula's no-account lawyer husband, and at the sight of him, Keith felt the blood drain from his cheeks.

"Rigby," Keith said, hand extended. "Good to see you."

"Keith," Rigby said, gripping his hand a little too hard, wearing a pink polo shirt and khaki pants and tasseled loafers. Bobby made a show of looking him up and down with disdain.

"I believe you've entered the premises under the regrettable misapprehension that this is the Ventura Yacht Club, sir," Bobby said in a pretty good William F. Buckley drone, and to Keith's surprise, Rigby laughed. He didn't think of Rigby as someone with a sense of humor about himself.

"Hah, yeah, I'm kind of dressed that way, aren't I?" He folded his arms across his chest—big weight lifter's forearms like Popeye's, veins striated and bulging.

The door opened again, and the cabdriver stepped in and stood there looking around for a second before his eyes landed on Bobby. "I should have known I was coming for you. Let's get a move on before your old lady starts worrying."

"I don't need a ride, my old pal Thurston Howell the Third here is going to take me home."

"Afraid I can't, Mister," Rigby said. "My chauffeur won't let me pick up strangers."

Bobby allowed him a phlegmy chuckle, then the cabbie took him by the arm and helped support him on the way to the door. Rigby nodded to Brenda and ordered a Beefeater and tonic, climbing onto a stool next to Keith.

"He's kind of an interesting old guy."

"Yeah, he's all right before he starts getting mean. I think you caught him right before he was about to turn."

"Here you go, sugar," Brenda said, sliding the drink in front of Rigby.

"Don't remember ever seeing you in here before," Keith said.

"Never been in. Always noticed it driving past, though. Nice old sign out front." The burly neon Quaker ringing a bell and the words TOWN CRIER in what were once bright red cursive letters, faded now to a flickering pink, were well-known landmarks to Venturans, even to the vast majority of them who had never stepped inside and would never dream of doing so.

"It has that going for it."

"I'm here because Paula thought this was where you hung out. Got something I wanted to run past you. There's something I didn't want to talk about over the phone."

He was about to say something else when Brenda came back over and replaced Keith's beer without asking. "How you doing, sugar?" she asked Rigby.

He swished the remaining ice, swallowed the rest of the drink and handed her the glass. "I would have another, if another were on offer."

She took the glass with a sidelong look at Keith. "I'm Brenda, by the way, since our mutual friend lacks the couth to introduce us."

"My friends call me Rigby."

"Oh, I'm sure we'll be friends," she said. They watched in silence as she made the drink and put it on the bar with as kittenish a look as Keith had ever seen on her face. When she headed down the bar to deal with the morose contingent at the south end, he took a drink of his fresh beer.

"You ever hit that?" Rigby asked, jerking his head in Brenda's direction. He watched her carefully, nodding ever so slightly.

"Never have."

Rigby rapped his knuckles on the bar to signal a change

of topic. "Paula says your grandfather's a painter. Been around Ventura County since forever."

"Yeah."

"Is he any good?"

"I think he is. He made a living doing commercial art and working on cartoons when my Mom was a kid."

"It just might be I've got a job for a painter. Someone who knows a thing or two about the local art scene."

"Like a commission?"

"Exactly. Can you give me his number?"

"Let me talk to him first. He's past ninety, gets a little bit prickly."

"Ninety? And he's still painting?" He hesitated, made a face. "He's still good? Hands steady?"

"Oh, yeah. It's about all he does anymore."

Rigby wrote a number down on a napkin and slid it along the bar to Keith. "Give me a call if he's interested."

Rigby shook his hand, paid for the drinks and left in a hurry. *I'd be in a hurry to get home, too, if I was married to Paula,* he thought.

Brenda propped her breasts on the bar and arched a carefully plucked eyebrow. "Now that is one good-looking, muscly man. He married?"

"He sure is, Bren. Sorry."

She made a regretful clicking sound and leaned back against the backbar. "Too bad."

Good thing, Keith thought, because Rigby was exactly the kind of guy she kept ending up with, and the fact that he had more money than most of the others didn't make him any better.

CHAPTER THIRTEEN

THE WIFE HADN'T CAUGHT on yet that the husband had lost patience with the entire process. He kept checking his phone, but Paula hadn't heard it vibrate, and she knew he was checking the time.

Her own phone had buzzed three times during the showing, and she had made herself a habit of never checking messages or texts until a showing was over. It was a matter of making the client think he or she was more important to her than anything else that might be going on in her life. She knew she might be missing something genuinely important—a call from school about a sick child, for example—but she believed it had served her well over the years. And today's prospects were a recently retired couple from Studio City. The baby boomers were a demographic that appreciated an unanswered phone when they were being catered to. They weren't on the hook yet, but she felt they were close to settling on a house. The husband was scowling less frequently than he had been on the first few outings, and the wife had gone from an expressionless passivity to commenting so frequently Paula sensed she was irritating the husband. This was not a bad thing; often one mate would get tired of the search and acquiesce to the first house that appealed to the other.

The texts were from Germaine.

BUY YOU LUNCH
Then:
CAFÉ ZEKE 1 PM
Then:
??????????

Paula texted her acceptance and got into the car. Germaine pronounced her name in the French manner and maintained a few continental affectations that had hardened into habits, but Paula had learned from Germaine's vengeful ex-husband that her real first name was Shirley and that she'd been born and raised in Louisville. If she wasn't much for socializing, she had the virtue of directness, and an invitation to a meal was usually a sign of favor.

Germaine was seated already when Paula got there, and rose for a kiss on either cheek. "Sit."

She was in her early seventies, her hair lacquered to the point of brittleness and frosted blond over an undercoat of unnatural black, her nails painted a bright tangerine shade, her makeup heavily and expertly applied, her cream-toned pantsuit creaseless and immaculate.

"I'M WORRIED ABOUT YOU," Germaine said as soon as the server had left the entrées. The salad course had been devoted to talk of Germaine's grandchildren and Paula's kids, and Paula knew better than to try to redirect the conversation before the boss was ready.

She was taken aback. "Worried about me? What for?"

"Your numbers are shit, Paula."

Unaccustomed to criticism from Germaine, who had been her mentor for more than fifteen years, she snapped. "I just found buyers for the Channel Drive murder house."

"Right, and that's the old Paula I know and love. But

that's one sale, not a trend, and you know your numbers are shit lately."

"I've been in a slump."

"Is everything okay at home?"

"Of course."

"I hear Rigby's practice took a big hit when Britt fell off that mountain."

Under attack, she felt a panicky need to regain some ground. "It was a crevasse. He fell into it, not off. And the firm wasn't hit that hard."

"Sugar, it's common knowledge in the legal community. Landon told me about it."

"Landon." Rigby liked to say that Landon got more senior ass than a toilet seat at an old folks' home, and she fought the temptation to set the old girl straight about her boy-friend. Not a productive conversational strategy, she told herself, more of a nuclear strike.

"So if there's a problem I want to know about it."

Paula took an initial bite of her salmon. Germaine was well into her squab and halfway done with her carrot purée. "No, there's nothing wrong."

"Because if there isn't some improvement, we're going to have to look into making some changes."

She stopped chewing the salmon and, with some diffi-culty, swallowed. "Are you threatening to fire me?"

"Don't be ridiculous. I might have to put you on a straight commission, though."

The pit of her stomach tingled unpleasantly and she took a sip of wine, tart and cool and suddenly depressing. "I understand," she said.

"Don't freak out, Paula. I think very highly of you, you know that, and if I didn't I wouldn't have called you aside, I would've kicked your ass to the curb. And I think you know that."

It was true. Paula had seen her do it half a dozen times, send underperforming agents out the door. Some of them prospered elsewhere, others vanished. "I appreciate it. I'll get out from under this." She took in another bite of salmon and let it melt on her tongue.

She skipped dessert and headed for the car, feeling like shit.

AFTER LUNCH, THE SINGLE glass of wine felt like three. Fucking typical Germaine, putting it all on Rigby. The worst part was the fact that she was right about him. Like her mother, her mentor had seen right through that glib façade right away, and she hadn't cared. And while they might understand his appeal on a surface level, and while they'd never say anything outright, all her friends thought she'd married badly.

Now, a couple of decades down the road from the thrilling start of it all, looking in on it from the outside herself, she was right with them. If not for the kids, she wished sometimes she could undo the whole thing in a second and go back to her twenties and tell Rigby to fuck off the day she met him. Or at least when he asked her to marry him.

SHE WAS TOO DISCOMBOBULATED to get anything useful done, so she went downtown to see a movie. Walking up Main toward the theater, just a block from Rigby's building, she saw that someone had dropped a succession of marshmallows onto the sidewalk in a row, like Hansel and Gretel leaving a trail leading back home. There were six or eight of them, and ants had started deconstructing them for removal to their nest before the seagulls could find and abscond with them.

The only movie that hadn't already started was one she

didn't want to see, but it didn't matter. Anything two hours long in a dark room would suffice; if it was especially bad she might enjoy dissecting it.

It was worse than she'd expected, a slow-moving weeper about a woman who loved an amnesiac man whose memory of their life together she tried with mixed results to jog. Exactly the kind of shit she hated, and she analyzed its every fault with grim pleasure. She wondered if the book it was based on was any smarmier than the movie or less so. She wondered, too, whether there was something wrong with her for hating this kind of thing so much when it was so closely aimed at her precise demographic. When at long last the male lead died, she snickered aloud.

Outside again, she found that it had rained during the show, and the pleasant smell rising from the concrete made her feel cleansed, her confidence returning. *Fuck Germaine, I'll get through this, and when I'm back on top, I'll move to the competition. Or open my own agency.*

It had rained hard enough to melt the abandoned marshmallows, and though ants still swarmed thereupon, most of them were mired in the sugary goo like an entomological La Brea Tar Pits. By the time she got to her car she'd forgotten about them.

CHAPTER FOURTEEN

RIGBY'S EYE WAS UNTUTORED, but the old man's talent and skill were easy to discern. The paintings on his walls ranged from seascapes to portraits to what Rigby took for abstractions, though they might have been ordinary household objects looked at from odd angles for all he could tell. He didn't want to ask the old fellow, who was reading the *L.A. Times* at his dinner table, studiously ignoring him as he made the circuit of the living and dining room walls. Despite the variousness of their subject matter, they were all clearly by the same assured hand.

"Who's the lady?" he asked of a portrait of a full-lipped, sultry-eyed woman, her blond hair pulled into a bun and holding a cigarette between her fingers. The vivid orange of the burning end of it had caught his eye before the woman's face, but there was a melancholy, soulful quality to her that struck him as deeply erotic.

"That's my late wife," he said, eyes still on the paper.

"Sorry."

"Don't be. She went nuts not long after I painted it. Found Jesus and spent the rest of her life making me miserable."

He couldn't think of an appropriate verbal response, so he nodded and moved down the wall to a painting of a cow standing in a field and looking with what seemed to Rigby pure hatred at the viewer. "That's an angry-looking cow."

"He's a steer. You'd be angry too."

"So you've always been a painter?"

He set his paper down on the table and folded it up. "I've done a lot of other things. Worked as a commercial artist, worked in cartoons for a while, painting backgrounds. Fred Flintstone's house, shit like that. Now that I'm retired, all I do is paint my own stuff."

"You're good at it."

"How do you know?"

"They look good to me."

"That and two dollars will get me a cup of coffee."

Rigby sat down across from the old man at the long oak table in the dining room. "Mr. Seghers, I wonder if you'd entertain a proposition."

"Might as well call me Will. The boy says you want to commission a picture. Portrait? You and the missus, maybe?"

"Not exactly. It's more of a copy of an existing picture."

Seghers raised an eyebrow. "A copy."

"You've been in the Ventura art scene for a long time, is what Keith says."

"Grew up in a house on Poli, right down the street from where Keith lives now. Apart from the war and a few years after it I've spent my whole life around here."

"So I guess you're familiar with a Russian painter, worked in Ojai, name of Kushik?"

His face went from curious to borderline threatening with remarkable speed, and looking at the thick, ropy tendons of his big hands, Rigby had to remind himself that the man was past ninety. "What about Kushik?"

"So you knew him?"

"I studied with him. We ended up on unfriendly terms."

"Unfriendly how?"

"Doesn't matter. I didn't speak to him from 1953 until the day he died."

"Is that so?"

"Fine painter, rotten human being."

"Right. Here's the thing. I have a client, an elderly client who's not really in possession of his faculties." He was struck with a sudden awareness of the need for tact. "I'm an attorney, I don't know if Keith mentioned that."

"He did, but I would have known anyway. You talk like one."

"This client, he's got an original Kushik."

"Good for him, that's worth a lot of scratch these days."

"Thing is, he wants to give it away. To his old prep school in the Midwest, wants to show he made something of himself when they didn't think he ever would. Of course every teacher and principal he ever had is six feet in the ground."

Seghers drummed his fingers on the chair's frame. "Seems to me it's his right to do that if it pleases him."

"Thing is, he doesn't remember he promised to give the thing away. It means the world to him, it was a gift to his late wife from Kushik's widow."

Seghers paused for a moment and finally took a seat. He leaned across the table. "Mr. Rigby, you don't appear to me to be a stupid man."

"Thanks."

"Do I look simple to you, then? Senile, maybe?"

"No, sir, you seem to be in remarkable shape for a man of, a man of your, uh, years."

He squinted at Rigby in a manner that suggested the younger man was about to be ejected, by force if necessary. "Then why don't you cut the shit and tell me what you're really up to."

"How's that?"

"You're full of beans. If you wanted to spare his tender feelings you could delay the gift until after he croaked."

Rigby cursed himself for underestimating him and not having a better story. "The transfer was scheduled for this year, the school's got some kind of ceremony planned."

"Mr. Rigby, I'm going to give you one more chance before I throw your ass out onto my lawn. You're asking me to be a party to a criminal enterprise, but you won't let on the nature of that enterprise, in fact you deny that any criminality is involved. Now I'm not involved yet, but I know there's some monkey business going on involving a phony Kushik. If you want me involved, level with me."

Seghers would have made a good lawyer. Rigby thought about it for a moment. After the Billy Knox debacle it might be good to be involved with someone smarter than himself rather than stupider. "I want to give the school the copy and keep the real thing. My client has no idea what it's worth."

Seghers shook his head. It made him look tired. "Not a chance in hell that'll work."

"Uh-huh. What makes you say that?"

"A real Kushik hits the market in a few years' time. It seems to be identical to one donated to this man's alma mater. The experts convene. Kushik never painted the same subject twice. The question of provenance comes up, the fake is exposed, questions get asked. You haven't thought this out. Now, why don't we start over."

AT FIVE-THIRTY IN THE morning when his phone started vibrating on the nightstand, Rigby was already awake, turning over in his mind all the complications inherent in the merging of his old plan and Seghers's newer, more complicated one. He glanced at the screen:

*I WANT MY 5 GEE BITCH I KNOW WERE YOU *&LIVE

It was from the same number in the 805. Rigby stared at the message with incredulity at the notion that that skinny little fucker Knox had the audacity to threaten his home and family. His lack of anxiety came from a sure knowledge that he was in a better position to do his newly minted enemy harm than the reverse. Ernie Norwin, the boozy dolt who'd suggested the fuckwit for the job, had laid out the whole situation for Rigby: the girlfriend in Moorpark, the occasional troubles with the law, the reckless bravery and relative trustworthiness. Ernie didn't know the nature of the job, but he still owed Rigby six hundred and fifty for getting his pay ungarnished on a child support beef, and he was grateful for any way of taking off pressure.

"There's his apartment," Ernie had said, scrawling a nearly unreadable address onto a cocktail napkin, on which he had already doodled a pair of breasts as well as a pretty decent rendering of a thick-veined penis about to enter a very hairy vagina. "If he's not there, he's in Moorpark with Magda."

It occurred to Rigby now that maybe he owed Ernie Norwin a broken jaw as well. But better to forget about that unsettled score, at least until Knox had been dealt with properly.

HE WASN'T GOING TO get back to sleep, so he got up and showered. Once he was dressed, he went to the kitchen to make some coffee and was startled to find both his daughters sitting at the kitchen table, eating cereal and reading the Ventura County edition of the *Times*.

"What are you girls doing up at this hour?"

They glanced at one another, and then Fiona said, "What

are *you* doing up at this hour? We're always up by five-thirty. You're usually still sleeping when we go to school."

"Why so early?"

"It's the only way we have time to read the paper."

"You're eleven years old."

"Almost twelve," Isolde said.

"So if you're eleven you shouldn't be informed?" Fiona said.

"I didn't say that."

"Who's the secretary of the Treasury?" Fiona asked.

"How should I know?"

Once again the girls exchanged glances, not bothering to hide their smirks. He filled the coffee maker with water and popped a pod into place, then hit the ON button.

"I guess this happens to everybody eventually. You wake up one morning and your kids know more than you do," he said. Neither of them contradicted him, and before his coffee was ready, they were both engrossin the paper again.

BY SIX-THIRTY, RIGBY WAS standing on Stony Flynn's doorstep on the outskirts of Ojai. Stony had made it known from the outset that he didn't approve of Rigby's direct involvement in the purchase of the purloined coke. "Not your world, brah," he'd said. "No offense, but you're a slick, legit guy, you're dealing with people unlike yourself. Put up the money and let someone else do the messy parts." Rigby planned to avoid the subject altogether if possible.

Stony opened the door, fully dressed in denim overalls over a yellow T-shirt with a hidden logo, and Rigby suspected that he hadn't been to bed yet. "Yo," he said, opening the door to let Rigby cross the threshold. "Have a seat."

Rigby sat down on a plain wooden chair next to a round table.

"You want some coffee?"

"If it's made, I wouldn't mind."

Stony nodded and limped into the kitchen, past a worn-out curtain made of old bedsheets, and hollered back into the living room. "You didn't see a polydactyl cat outside, did you?"

"A what?"

"Cat with thumbs, basically."

"No." An overwhelming feline odor hung over the little house, an overflowing litter box sat in the corner, and all over the room were mounds of laundry, though it was impossible to tell which mounds were clean and which were dirty. Rigby had been surprised one day a month earlier when Stony's wife showed up in her blue scrubs after a shift at the animal hospital; he'd assumed that only a single man could live like that.

He came back into the living room and set two mugs down on the bare, scarred wood of the table, then sat across from Rigby. The big man was splendidly hirsute; he shaved every day above his jawline, but it had been years since razor or scissors had touched a hair below it, and the locks flowing from his throat were luxuriant and curly.

"How'd your operation go?"

"Fine."

He nodded, hard and only once. "Good."

They sat for a minute in silence, and finally Rigby gave in and spoke first. "I need a gun."

Stony held his gaze for an uncomfortably long moment, and Rigby had to concentrate hard in order not to avert his eyes. "Operation went good, you said."

"This is something else."

"Uh-huh." His expression didn't change, and he didn't inquire further, just sat there staring at Rigby.

"So, obviously, one that won't get traced back to you."

"I've got one that'll do you. Three hundred dollars. Best I can do."

"Kind of steep, isn't it?"

"Not when you consider the amount of risk I'm taking personally."

"Didn't I just ask for a gun can't be traced back to you?"

"You did, and this one can't, at the moment. Once you've used it, though, there's a trail leads back to me."

"You don't think I'd give you up if I got caught, do you?"

"I don't have any basis to judge. You seem like a smart man, and you helped me out on a couple of occasions, so I owe you. But I'll tell you once again, you're a well-educated, well-off man, a lawyer, and this kind of shit is not where your expertise lies."

Rigby had been prepared to pay five hundred. He opened his wallet and pulled out three Benjamins. Stony leaned across the table, nodding once with a grunt that might have been an acknowledgment that a deal had been struck, or might have been an expression of the exertion of leaning.

Then he stood and headed for the kitchen. "I'll go fetch it, then. But I still advise against it. You bring this gun back to me unfired, and I'll give you your money back."

"How will you know if I've fired it or not?"

Stony turned to face him. "I'll look in your eyes," he said before disappearing through the vertical bedsheets.

RIGBY SAT IN HIS poor dead buddy Britt's Denali on a side street perpendicular to a darkened Moorpark street, with a nice view of the row of dingy apartments above the frilly dresses and spangled party favors in the quinceañera supply place beneath them. It was 11 P.M., the store and its neighbors all closed for the night, and if the other apartments were occupied they showed no sign of it. There wasn't much in the way of foot traffic, either, the orange streetlights glowing on empty pavement and the occasional passing sedan.

He didn't feel in the least agitated, not even with the gun holstered underneath his sport jacket, not knowing whether or not he'd be called upon to use it. By eleven-thirty, though, he was bored, and he lacked the patience to sit there all night until Knox and his girlfriend came home from whatever glue-sniffing donkey show they were at.

Beth still used Britt's Denali for certain tasks calling for its hauling capability, which made Rigby feel a little weird in the same way that fucking her in Britt's bedroom did— why not trade the thing in and get another one that hadn't belonged to a dead person? It was the same reason he got the heebie-jeebies around people wearing vintage clothing. Paula came home once from an estate sale with a fifties-era dress she thought he'd find sexy, and the thought still made him shudder. "The person who used to wear that is dead," he said. "Of course she is, it was an estate sale. Don't you want to fuck me in it?" she'd asked, puzzled and hurt. *Jesus, Paula.*

Now, though, he'd found an upside to Beth's continued use of the SUV. On the seat was a big plastic bag containing various sorts of office supplies, leftover tools of whichever volunteer job she'd been working that afternoon.

He put the Denali into gear and drove around to the alley behind the apartments. Already wearing latex gloves because of the gun, he climbed up the fire escape to the second story and tried the door. It was locked, but its paint was flaking and the wood around the knob looked ready to crumble, so he took a step back and put his shoulder into it. There came a satisfying, promising crack, and he stepped back and shoved again, harder. This time it gave, sending splinters of rotten wood into the dark hallway.

He couldn't find a light switch, but the streetlight outside was sufficiently bright for him to see the name SCHULLER written in punch-out tape underneath the letter B on one of the doors. That would be Ms. Magda Schuller, Knox's girlfriend. Underneath it, he put one of Beth's Post-its, with a message printed in Magic Marker:

I FOUND YOU

CHAPTER FIFTEEN

"WHAT IF WE JUST stopped trying to act like we're rich?" she asked. She hadn't really meant to say it out loud, but there it was, hanging in the air.

Rigby turned his head to face her directly. It was a perfectly straight stretch of road through Carpinteria where Santa Claus Lane used to be, but it drove her crazy when he took his eyes off the freeway.

"Jesus, Rigby, watch the goddamn road."

"What do you mean?"

"The road!"

"About acting like we're rich?"

"I mean, what if we lived in a smaller house? Took the kids out of St. Aloysius and put them in public school?"

He looked gobsmacked, but at least his eyes were back on the freeway. He shook his head and let out a breath. "This is a hell of a time to be letting me know I'm a failure as a breadwinner."

"Oh, cut the bullshit. You know that's not it."

"First of all, we *are* rich. I'm going through a fallow period is all."

"We both are. Forget I said anything, I was just thinking maybe it wasn't so great that we had a strong ten-year run and got used to it."

"Baby, the difference between you and me is you see the glass half empty and I see it full."

"That's not the way the analogy works."

"Tonight you're going to meet Glenn's girl Nina and you're going to get an idea how much money we're going to make." He looked over at her again, but just for a second this time, and despite herself she felt a moment's consolation. Fucking Rigby. He always managed to talk her into buying whatever soap he was selling.

THE BOOTH THEY WERE in was dark, but it was still daylight outside. Dinner with Glenn Haskill and his assistant, or nurse, or whatever she was, was at five-thirty, so Paula just ordered a glass of wine and a side salad. When Glenn objected, as she'd known he would, she smiled sweetly and explained that she was on a diet. The expressionless creature beside him arched an eyebrow at the assertion.

"You don't need to be on a diet."

"I'm maintaining. The food here's pretty rich."

"You don't come to Arnoldi's for your health," Glenn said.

They'd brought the old boy in with the aid of a walker, trailing an oxygen canister on wheels. It had taken a good fifteen minutes from Glenn's car to the booth, all three of them taking tiny steps to match his shuffling gait and trying to make it look natural. Now the old goat sat there in his purple velour smoking jacket and his ascot and his pencil mustache, weighing 130 pounds and talking about pussy as though they were four men at the table, and arrested adolescents at that. The assistant joined in, but not in an approving or disapproving way; she seemed to regard her employer as a scientific subject.

"How much did you promise these women before they had sex with you? A single episode? A recurring role?" she said.

"I didn't have to promise them anything at all. And don't think they didn't have a good time in the sack themselves. They were gambling. Throwing the dice they'd get work out of it."

"You mean you didn't even give them jobs?"

Glenn shrugged and scowled. "Not every single one. But if she was a decent lay, I'd let it be known she was looking for work."

"Did any of them ever get famous?" Rigby asked. It seemed to Paula that he actually admired this aspect of Haskill's life.

"Not a one. One girl, I remember, went back to Wichita and used to send me a Christmas card every year without fail. Another one got involved with a movie director, damn near broke up his marriage till the wife came after her with a gun. That made the *Herald Examiner* and the *Times* both, she was the only one I thought might have made it. Scandal ruined her, though. Overdosed on Seconal a year or so after that. Once in a while I'd see one of 'em in Hughes or Mrs. Gooch's or someplace, and they'd step up and say hello. Or I'd run into one cocktail waitressing in a short skirt in Tarzana. A couple I know for sure ended up turning tricks. This girl Trixie, that's how long ago this was, weren't any Trixies after about 1960, were there? Anyway, Trixie'd quit acting and I heard she was working as a call girl, back about '67, '68, I remember because *Garrigan* was still on the air, so I booked a suite at the Beverly Hills Hotel and had her come over. She was absolutely wonderful. One of the best pieces of ass I've ever had in my life, to this day. And afterward she asked me if I might give her a small part on *Garrigan*. A call girl!"

Rigby shook his head in shared wonderment at the brazen gall of Trixie the call girl wanting to get back into acting. Haskill's companion betrayed no response.

She'd been wondering whether Rigby was sleeping with this assistant he kept talking about, but seeing her she doubted it. With her big round glasses and her bangs, she wasn't his physical type; watching them interact in front of her, she decided they were too familiar and careless to be guilty of anything. Rigby might not have a conscience, and he was an accomplished liar, but around Paula, he treated Beth Warden with a chilly indifference that all but announced a secret, shameful intimacy.

As she nibbled on her salad and the other three gorged on pasta, even poor emaciated Glenn, he continued to regale them with tales of crass behavior and casual cruelty. She had always liked the old fellow, and she still did, but the more he talked, the more comfortable she felt with the idea of robbing him.

WHEN THE MEAL WAS over, Rigby suggested that the assistant ride with Paula in the Escalade. "I'll drive Glenn in his, we've got a few business details to go over. You'd be bored stiff."

"Sure. It's a good ten minutes back to the house, that's way too long to take that kind of skull-numbing tedium," the woman said as she climbed into the passenger side of the Escalade. "It was my idea," she told Paula as they drove toward the 101.

"Beg pardon?"

"Faking the Kushik."

"I guess I owe you, then."

"I hear you found us a painter."

She merged onto the freeway. Traffic was light for that time of the evening, the low sun casting a nectarine shade onto the mountains. "I don't know how good he is."

"Rigby says he knew Kushik, that'll be enough. Jesus, look

at him drive." She indicated Haskill's Lincoln, weaving in and out of the carpool lane.

"Is he texting?" Paula said. She sped up and pulled along-side, expecting to see Rigby at the wheel, but her husband was in the passenger seat and old Glenn drove, gesticulating wildly as he cackled his way through some other filthy anec-dote. Rigby looked about as scared as she'd ever seen him, but he was laughing gamely in spite of the grave physical peril he'd placed himself in.

A FEW MINUTES LATER, they were gathered in what had been Evvie Haskill's parlor, having an after-dinner drink and examining the Haskills' collection of antiques. Paula was grateful for the alcohol, the antiques being less than astonishing. A taxidermied owl, its beak sadly splintered, looked down on the proceedings from a perch made from a birch branch. Some of its feathers had been rubbed away to reveal bumpy, leathery skin.

"You see this?" Haskill said, holding up a fancifully deco-rated piece of porcelain. "It's a chamber pot from Windsor Castle. I bought it in an auction twenty years ago." He spoke of it with a pride other men reserved for grandchildren.

"What'd it set you back?" Rigby said.

"I'd have to look it up, but it was a pretty penny, believe you me. One of the few big antique buys Evvie and I ever agreed on." He held the delicate vessel at arm's length and admired it. "Just think, Queen Victoria herself squatted on this thing and took a shit."

"I feel like I'm in the very presence of royalty," Nina said, which earned her a brief, sharp glance from her employer, who quickly softened, probably because her expression was so carefully neutral it was impossible to tell whether she was being sarcastic.

Haskill and Rigby sat down at an old desk that the old man claimed had belonged to William S. Hart and was therefore worth many tens of thousands of dollars, overestimating, perhaps, the number of remaining William S. Hart fans still haunting the antique market in search of relics to worship. They were examining some first-day covers from the 1960s, most of them commemorating events in the space program. Rigby was doing a valiant job of pretending to care, asking for details about the nature of this or that Apollo mission, feigning interest in which astronauts had actually set foot on the moon and which ones had had to settle for orbiting the thing.

Nina tugged at her silk sleeve and jerked her head toward the hallway. They slipped out of the room and down the hallway to a room Paula had never entered, upon whose wall hung a picture of a little girl.

"This is it," Nina said.

"It's worth how much?"

"It'll save your house and then some."

She found herself pissed off that Rigby had told her about the house being underwater. "So our guy paints a copy and no one can tell the difference."

"Rigby didn't tell you? Plan's changed."

"He doesn't tell me shit, that's how we got into the mess we're in."

"Kushik never painted the same subject twice, so if the real thing and a copy were both out there we'd be found out. So your painter's going to paint a portrait of somebody else."

She leaned in close and peered at the thick blobs of paint. It was a pretty picture, but she couldn't see it being worth enough to save their house. "I wonder where this little girl is now."

"My best guess is this was painted in Taos around 1935, so if she's alive she's in her late eighties."

"She looks so sad."

"Everybody in Kushik's pictures does. Come on, let's get back to the stamp show before Mr. Haskill notices."

CHAPTER SIXTEEN

LEISURE AUTO SALES AND Leasing of St. Louis County was one of those places like the St. Louis Country Club or Creston School, places where Jerry felt judged harshly for having slid so far economically from the lofty perch he was born on. He felt that way even dealing with people who didn't know and probably wouldn't care about his precarious situation. He dreaded the reaction of the sales rep, an inveterate snob named Wesley Brickell who owned a good chunk of the dealership; he'd already sneered eight months ago when Jerry downgraded from an LX to an NX. At any rate Jerry thought he'd detected a sneer.

"I need out of my lease."

"Swapping up or down?"

"Out. I'm going through a rough patch." His throat tightened just admitting it.

"Listen, we can work something out." He got up from his desk and crossed around to where Jerry sat, placed a consoling hand on his shoulder. "It can't be that bad. Why don't we get you into something with a lower monthly?"

He shook his head. "I really need to get out from under it."

"Jer, I want to help out any way I can. My dad and yours were friends for decades."

This wasn't quite true. Their dads had been coevals and social peers, but his own dad didn't really have friends so to speak, spending all his time and energy on his oddball, solitary hobbies. "I appreciate it, Wes, but I just want out."

Wes's expression took on a harder tone. "There's a penalty for breaking the lease. Big chunk of your deposit."

"I know." He was choking again, his voice catching shamefully. "I was hoping you could cut me a break."

"I'll see what I can come up with." Wes sat back down again. "Let me ask Pete Maloney what I can do."

"Jesus, the whole 'let me ask my manager' routine? I thought you owned the place."

Wes frowned. "I have partners. And this will have to come out of my end."

He sat there shrinking into the deep leather chair as Wes detailed his woes over the phone to Pete Maloney, who'd been a couple of years behind him at Creston. Pete had been a football player, not quite a star but good enough to make him a popular kid, and he'd gone on to several careers, each one a little more successful than the previous. He was still married to his first wife and had four kids, all of them at college or recently graduated. He was living exactly the life everyone had expected Jerry to live, and now he sat on the other end of the line listening to the broad outlines of Jerry's ignominious failure.

AT SEVEN THAT NIGHT he was behind the wheel of a 1999 Olds Cutlass that belonged to his mother, sailing east on 64. He'd taken a bath on the penalty, but he was out from under the fucking onerous monthly payments, and his stress level was so close to normal now that he was sailing past other drivers without even cursing them under his breath. He thought he could actually feel his lowered blood pressure in his scalp.

His problem at the moment was that, driving the Cutlass, he couldn't show up at any of his usual watering holes without inviting questions, or worse, pity, from his cronies. Not that he had many left.

But he hadn't been to the Loop in a while, and though surely the offerings would have changed up there would still be bars. He turned off Skinker and onto Delmar and immediately began rumbling on some goddamned obstacle or another. It was darker than he'd realized, and when he put his headlights on, he saw that he was driving on railroad tracks. *That fucking trolley.* Last time he'd been down here, it was still talk; now the tracks were laid, fucking up suspensions and wrecking bicycles. All for an exercise in nostalgia that didn't even go anywhere, just up and down the street for show.

Parking was scarce, but on a hunch he turned into the movie theater lot and grabbed a space just as it opened up. After a minute standing at the solar-powered meter that served the whole lot, trying in vain to figure out its interface, he gave up, figuring he could afford to risk a fifteen-dollar parking ticket. He was broke, but he wasn't destitute yet. Directly across the street was the site of one of his old favorite taverns, replaced by something cleaner and probably nicer, and instead of mourning the old place he jaywalked straight over to the replacement.

The crowd was a mix of young and old, and he didn't see anyone he knew. He took a seat at the bar and watched a Cardinals game. It was the first in a long time he'd paid any attention to, and he wondered how his once-intense interest in baseball had faded. He hadn't been particularly conscious of it as it happened, but one year as the playoffs neared, he realized he hadn't been to a single game. Now he didn't even watch them on TV, barely glancing at the standings in the *Post-Dispatch* unless they were at the top of the division and headed for the post-season.

He was on his third Bushmills when he saw Mrs. Kimball, whatever her first name was, seated at a table with two other women about her own age. He looked away, not really in the mood to talk to strangers, but at a second glance he recognized one of her companions as a social studies teacher he'd gone out with a few times before marrying Valerie. It couldn't hurt to stop over and say hello.

What was Mrs. Kimball's first name? He must have heard it when he met her. For that matter, what was the social studies teacher's name? He remembered that her canary's name was Petey, and he remembered her address, at least the one she'd had when they dated, but the first and last name remained buried amid the detritus and trivia of his memory banks.

He rose and approached their table with an ambitiously friendly grin. They all stopped talking and looked up at him, slightly puzzled. "Sorry," he said to Mrs. Kimball. "We met at the auction. Your husband's director of development, right?"

"Oh," she said. "Trey and Belinda's friend. With the uncle in California."

"Jerry Haskill," the social studies teacher said, her voice and expression carefully neutral.

He extended his hand, suddenly aware that this was not proper protocol for greeting someone with whom you'd had intimate physical contact. "It's nice to see you."

She took his hand, smirking, gave it a slight shake and then withdrew her own.

"Wells was just talking about your uncle yesterday," Mrs. Kimball said. "He found an article in *Connoisseurship Magazine* about Kushik."

"Who?"

"The painting your uncle's planning on gifting to the school."

"What's his name again?" He really didn't want to be reminded about his uncle's plans to give the school money, and made a mental note to call the sleazebag lawyer in the morning to see if together they could forestall any rewriting of the old boy's will. Surely Rigby objected to the idea as much as he did.

"Kushik."

The third woman looked up at Jerry as though something had just surprised her. "Wait a minute, Bar, is this the Jerry you went out with before Trevor?"

Bar! The social studies teacher's name was Barbara. She was suppressing a laugh, but she nodded, and the third woman snorted and then guffawed, leaving Mrs. Kimball embarrassed. "I'll be sure to tell Wells that I saw you," she said, looking askance at her friends.

Jerry nodded and, sensing that a second chance with Bar was not in the offing, excused himself and returned to his stool, watching the three women in the mirror. Bar and the third woman were stifling giggles as they told Mrs. Kimball tales of some sort. She reacted with wide-eyed disbelief at whatever they were telling her, occasionally cracking up herself, covering her mouth with her hands and, once, glancing into the mirror and for the briefest of seconds meeting his gaze before looking down.

IN THE MORNING, HE called Rigby's office and got the sour-voiced old woman who worked for him. "He's not here. I'll leave him a message, but I can't tell you when he'll get back to you. He's not in the office much these days."

"It's important."

"Listen, hon, I'm sure it is. I spend all day trying to get him to pay attention to important things, but his idea of important doesn't necessarily mesh with yours or mine, if you know what I mean."

He had been dealing with Rigby long enough to know this. "Okay, can you tell him I need to talk to him? And it's urgent?"

"I'll put you on his call list."

After hanging up, he made himself a third cup of coffee and turned the TV on. He struggled with the remote's confusing new interface until he got to the Channel Guide and found, to his delight, that an episode of *High Cimarron* had started. He settled back and comforted himself with the notion that each rerun brought his uncle a little bit more money that would one day be his, unless it went to that goddamn school.

CHAPTER SEVENTEEN

WILL SEGHERS WALKED INTO the Town Crier to meet with his grandson. Instead he found Rigby, dressed like a slumming yachtsman in a bright green Polo shirt and cargo shorts, deep in conversation with Brenda, who looked downright infatuated.

Keith had told him Rigby had come into the bar looking for him, and this concerned him. He'd been coming here since the fifties and considered it home, and he didn't like Rigby and didn't want him becoming a regular. He certainly didn't want the slick son of a bitch to start thinking they were friends.

"There he is!" Rigby yelled, and a pair of sullen, pipe-cleaner-thin rubes looked up at Will from their game of pool. A few stools on the other side of Rigby sat Clay Chute, a doughy, bearded software engineer, staring mournfully at the back of Brenda's head while she sliced a plastic tray of limes, his crush as painful to watch as it must have been for him to live through. Will sometimes thought about bringing the subject up with him, counseling him against the folly of getting all emotionally worked up about a woman he wasn't actually involved with, but poor Chute was careful never to explicitly acknowledge his infatuation. There were a few couples and old folks in the booths, and another skinny country boy with a long, cornsilk blond ponytail stood over the jukebox, picking at his teeth with his forefinger and studying the titles with Talmudic concentration.

"Mr. Rigby," Will said. Assuming the man had come to talk business, he sat down next to him. Brenda put the tray of limes in its designated spot and approached them.

"Now there's a man with a handsome white head of hair," she said, placing a coaster in front of him.

"Bless you, child."

"Glad you came in, pal." Rigby looked over his shoulder at the jukebox loiterer. "Numbnuts there just put on Styx and Billy Ray Cyrus one right after the other." His voice was louder than strictly necessary.

"Now, let's not go ragging on other people's personal taste," Brenda said. "It's not the world's best-stocked jukebox."

Will kept a discreet eye on the man at the jukebox to see if he was listening.

"Jesus, you can say that again," Rigby said. "That's the only thing I don't like about coming here so far, the seventies hair music and the shitty country oldies."

Right then, "Achy Breaky Heart" finished and "God Bless the U.S.A." by Lee Greenwood came on in its place.

"Oh, fuck me, he's got to be putting us on." If the beanpole hadn't heard that, he couldn't miss what came next: Rigby, singing along with the record in a loud, high-pitched, moronic voice. "Whur it Laist Ah Knowum Fraaaay!"

"Okay, enough," Will said, motioning for him to turn down the volume.

"Sssshhh, now," Brenda said, an expression of motherly indulgence on her face that was more likely to egg Rigby on than to quiet him. Will fervently hoped he wasn't going to have to warn her away from him, but her gaze was one of near adoration, and he'd seen that look augur bad fortune for her before.

One of the pool-playing ectomorphs approached the bar, and when Brenda went to take his order, Rigby leaned over. "So. Timewise. You're an artist, you work when you get inspired, I get it. But just as a hypothetical, how long is this picture going to take?"

"Ten days," he said. It was an exaggeration, but it would give him negotiating room.

"Make it two," Rigby said.

"Five. I want a deal on paper."

"Normally that's not something you do when you're planning something illegal."

"I've been screwed enough times in the art business that I want protection. You're a lawyer, you can figure something out."

RIGHT THEN THE PONYTAILED scarecrow came over from the jukebox and yanked at the back of Rigby's polo shirt. His upper teeth hung out so far ahead of the lower set that Will wondered how the man managed to swallow liquids.

"You don't like the music I put on?"

Rigby seemed to have forgotten about the jukebox and its discontents, and he spun to greet the man. "Sorry, what?"

"I said maybe you ought to keep your faggot opinions to your fuckin' self," he said, a little drop of spittle flying from his lips, and he gave Rigby an ineffective shove.

Rigby stood, grabbed the ponytail with his right hand and smashed the man's forehead against the bar molding with considerable force. Skinny went down with a look of considerable surprise on his face, hitting his head again on the floor. Brenda screamed, and the pool players looked at each other with their mouths open. They put down their cues and sidled like bipedal, undernourished crabs to the exit.

There was a bloody gash in the vanquished man's

forehead, and he was having trouble keeping his eyes focused on the rubber feet of the barstool six inches from his face. Brenda, her infatuation with Rigby crossing her wires, came to the counterintuitive conclusion that Will was the one who needed a dressing-down.

"Goddamn it," she shouted, finger pointed at Will's nose. "Your friend here's eighty-sixed!"

"You're eighty-sixed, I guess," he said to Rigby.

"What?" he said, looking, with his bright green shirt, gritted teeth and massive clenched fists, just like the Incredible Hulk. "You saw. He was trying to pick a fight."

A FEW MINUTES AFTER Rigby left, Keith showed up and took his place. As Will told him about Rigby's misbehavior, the lad blanched and got very quiet.

"I'm starting to wonder if your friend Rigby's playing with all his marbles," Will said.

"Yeah."

"You're not too talkative tonight. Something bothering you?"

"Gramps, do you remember once when we were here visiting, I was about five or six, and you brought me here for a Seven Up?"

The old man stared straight ahead, squinting, then turned back to him. "'Brought you here' as in 'here to the bar'? Like hell I did."

"You took me to see *Ghostbusters II*, and afterward you said, 'Hey, boy, how'd you like a Seven Up?' So anyway, can I ask you a question?"

"If I could think of a way to prevent you doing it, I would."

"The lady behind the bar, long white hair. Took a liking to me. Gave me a bag of beer nuts. Sat there caressing my cheek with the back of her hand while I ate."

Will slapped the bar. "Yeah, I do remember that day. She took quite a shine to you."

"I remember she told me to call her Susie."

"That was her name all right. Her hair wasn't white, it was platinum blond. You have a better memory than most. She would have been late forties, maybe early fifties then, just about hitting her prime. Kind of woman who starts off average and gets better with the passing years, if you know what I mean. What's your question?"

"So when we left and headed back to the house you said, 'Let's not tell Gram about stopping for the Seven Up, okay?'"

"Nothing unusual about a man wanting to keep his wife in the dark about an afternoon visit to the local watering hole."

"I just had this feeling that Susie was your girlfriend. I don't know why I thought that. She had quite a figure, didn't she? Nice cleavage."

"Exactly what the hell kind of pervert six-year-old meets a woman of fifty and judges her tits?"

"Anyway, I was determined to keep your secret."

His grandfather let out a low rumble of a laugh. "Much appreciated."

"Grandma wasn't a lot of fun, was she?"

Will saw that there was guilt in speaking that thought out loud, even though his wife had never liked the boy much. Little Keith had been a bit too loud, a bit too rambunctious, a bit too prone to trying outdoor activities like wiffle ball indoors.

"No she wasn't, not by the time you were born. Thirty or so years earlier, she wasn't half bad. It was religion that ruined her, going to work at that fucking church. All of a sudden, everything I did was going to land me in the lake of fire."

"So whatever happened to Susie?"

He squinted and looked up at the ceiling. "Her son moved to Georgia or Tennessee and had a couple kids, she moved out there to be close to them. That must be at least twenty years ago. She could be a great-grandma now, I suppose."

"Was she single?"

"Divorced by that time."

"You ever have anything going on with a married woman?"

Will pulled his head up and back, and his eyes brightened. "That's how come you're having trouble with that girlfriend of yours. You're topping a married lady on the side. One of your students, I bet."

Keith took a sip of his beer.

"Don't they make you fellows take an oath?"

Keith looked away, down the bar to where Brenda stood. She was looking at him, and gave him a little wave.

"Let me guess, whatever's the matter has something to do with the married lady. Or her husband."

"I don't think I want to talk about it right now."

"Suit yourself. Just seems to me if you didn't want to talk, you could have had a beer at home."

Keith scratched at the corner of the label on his bottle and started peeling it away from the brown glass. "The lady I've been seeing. I'm a little concerned about her husband finding out and his reaction being violent or maybe homicidal."

His grandfather waved a big, gnarled paw across his face. "You're being dramatic. Most guys haven't landed a punch since grade school. You're an athlete, he's probably some deskbound doughball who wouldn't hurt a fly."

Keith nodded at the ponytailed man with the gash on his head, a wet towel pressed to it stained with red. "Tell that guy about it."

"Rigby did that, he's crazy. Your gal's husband is incapable of any such thing, trust me."

"You're slow on the uptake tonight, Gramps."

"Wait one minute."

Keith nodded.

"Sheee-it."

CHAPTER EIGHTEEN

ON THE DRIVE HOME from the Town Crier, a sense of placid well-being settled over Rigby. Not that he didn't regret the little outburst of violence, but it was entirely the other guy's fault, intruding on his space and calling him names. Of course, the main reason he'd felt compelled to mock the man's musical taste was the fact that he reminded Rigby of Billy Knox, so maybe he did share in some of the blame himself.

Fucking Knox's fault, if you thought about it, for getting him all keyed up in the first place. Another message had come that afternoon, from the unnamed 805 number.

FIND ME AGAN IF YOU CAN BEFORE U DEAD AND GIMME MY 5TOUSAND.

Shit, he hadn't put any kind of scare into the little bastard at all. He should have nailed a dead squirrel to the girlfriend's door; that would have sent a message. Now he was going to have to find him again.

He slowed down as he approached the Shanty. Maybe he could talk to Norwell again. He'd surely know by now about the bad blood between Rigby and Knox, but he might talk for money, and Rigby still had a pair of new hundred-dollar bills in his wallet, enough to buy a guy like Norwell a lot of crank and Keystone Light.

Pulling into the lot, though, he saw Knox's beater of a pickup, an old Toyota with no rear hatch and three different panel colors besides the original red, faded now to a dull matte pink. He backed out and parked half a block down Main, with a good view of the front door, wishing he was in Beth's Denali again. If Knox was drunk, though—and Rigby suspected he would be—he wouldn't notice the Lexus tailing him quietly back to wherever his spider hole was.

He called home, just in case this took all night. "Look, I'm going to be late. Working on another draft of Haskill's will."

"Suit yourself." It bothered him a little that she didn't put up any resistance. It might be nice if she were a little jealous, just for the sake of his ego, although he supposed that would make his gallivanting more complicated. She took him for granted, though, didn't even consider the possibility he might be out for some strange. Admittedly, tonight he was stalking someone with violent intent rather than philandering, but the principle was the same.

He was about to call Beth to check on her availability later in the evening—her kids' school was on a four-day break, and there was a decent chance they were with friends overnight—but just as he was about to make the call the front door of the Shanty opened and Knox stepped outside, his gait uncertain and his face sullen. He got into his truck and, after a minute or so fumbling with the ignition, managed to get it started, then headed north on Main. Feeling touched by something akin to a state of grace, Rigby started following.

THERE WASN'T MUCH TRAFFIC on the old Ojai road, but Rigby imagined Knox was sufficiently shit-faced not to notice that the same set of headlights had been behind him all the way from the Shanty. When the pickup turned off onto a side road just after the old barn converted into a farmers market, Rigby sailed on past it before turning off his headlights and making a U-turn. Knox's taillight—there was only one working—was about a quarter mile ahead of him, and all over the road, as he had been since leaving the bar. It was a good thing that Knox hadn't been spotted by a cop, because that would have put the son of a bitch in jail overnight, and who knew where he'd land after that.

Two miles up the road Knox turned left onto what looked like a private road, and once again Rigby drove past the turnoff, watching the truck slow and finally stop. He parked the Lexus on the side of the road and put on a pair of latex gloves, then took the gun from its spot under the seat. He closed the door as quietly as possible, then walked up to the trees that mostly blocked his view of the truck.

Knox stood there with the truck's headlights aimed at the front door of a big ranch-style house. He was laughing and singing something Rigby couldn't make out, and at length he went inside the house without turning the headlights off, the careless, stupid motherfucker.

A light went on in one of the front windows. It was a nice house, not new but expensive and well kept. What the hell was Knox doing in such a place? He hoped whoever really lived there wasn't inside. But there were no other cars, and he doubted that the owners were the kind to consort willingly with the likes of Billy Knox.

Through the window he saw Knox settle down into a big chair and close his eyes, still singing, giggling a little. His mouth didn't open for either function. Rigby tried the front door. Finding it unlocked, he opened it with great care.

He stood there in the living room, illuminated by the truck lights, the gun heavy in his hand. He watched Knox sitting there in the big comfy overstuffed armchair, singing and giggling still, jaw wired shut. "Fishiesh inna itty-bitty pooool."

"Knox." *Look at this moron.* No self-control. No fear, either, he was too stupid to feel it. There was no way to talk sense to a man like that. No way to trust that such a man wouldn't use what he knew about Rigby against him.

"Three lil fishiesh inna . . ." It was going to have to come to this eventually. It would be stupid to waste such an opportunity; he might never get another this perfect.

"Knox," he said, louder this time, and Knox opened his eyes, squinting against the lamplight.

"The fuck?" is all he managed to get out before Rigby fired, hitting him in the chest. The sound itself was ungodly, the echo just as bad. Jesus, he should have asked Stony about a silencer or something, his ears were going to be ringing for a week.

He approached Knox to see if he was dead, but before he got close enough to say for sure he turned to face a female figure standing in a doorway, one that must have led to a bedroom, since she was wearing only a bra and panties that didn't match. She was pudgy and pale, piebald with freckles, her long red hair in a topknot, and as her groggy mind struggled with the scene before her she began to wail in sorrow and terror. He fired at her, too, twice in rapid succession, hitting her in the chest with both rounds, and she fell backward, and then she was on the floor, blood pooling beneath her and into the grout between the granite tiles. With his hand over his agonizing right ear he checked on Knox, who looked just as dead as his lady friend.

"Teach you to threaten your betters, you ignorant hillbilly prick. Went and got your girlfriend killed too."

He felt a wave of nausea, but fought it back with the

thought that vomit might contain DNA, and anything he had to clean up would mean more time spent here, and more chances to leave behind some other kind of evidence. He reached into Knox's right-front pocket and extracted a cell phone. He checked the address book and found it empty, and the call history listed not a single incoming or outgoing call. Just three texts seemed to have been sent from the phone, all of them to Rigby's own. As long as he took it away from the scene there was nothing to tie it to Knox.

He exited the house and walked back out to the dirt road, thinking about confession the next morning. This was the worst thing he'd ever had to get absolution for, especially when you considered the girlfriend, who didn't have much to do with his and Knox's beef. He wondered which parish would be the best for an A-one serious, double Fifth Commandment–breaking cardinal sin. Maybe this was one he should keep to himself, or between himself and the Almighty.

Quickly, he ran through any mistakes he might have made, but the act had ended up being so simple he couldn't think of any faux pas. The ground was dry, so no tracks. He had latex gloves on, and the ballistics on the gun wouldn't lead anywhere if Stony was telling the truth—and Stony had a lot to lose if he was lying. Only Norwell could tie him to Knox now, and Norwell was a shitheel peckerwood imbecile with a police record.

It wasn't perfect, but Rigby knew enough cops and prosecutors and defense attorneys to know that no one was going to give this one the attention it would require to close it. Despite the adrenaline rush, he'd sleep soundly tonight.

But first he needed a release. He got out his phone and dialed Beth's number. It was two in the morning, later than he'd thought, and he knew that on waking up, she'd be pissed off. Didn't matter.

CHAPTER NINETEEN

HE CALLED PAULA EARLY in the morning, frantic and cryptic, unwilling to discuss anything on the phone and demanding a face-to-face. "It's not a sex thing. I need to talk to you about something else."

"You can talk all you want, Keith," she said, "but if I have to go to the trouble of arranging a private place, then it's going to be a sex thing."

The address she settled on was a furnished bungalow in Ojai, courtesy of a sympathetic colleague. When he arrived, he found Paula painting her toenails a bright shade of orange, the hard oak floor protected by the previous Sunday's Ventura County edition of the *L.A. Times*. "I got here half an hour early, thought I'd take advantage," she said. The left foot was done and she was hard at work on the right, and he found himself ogling her lovely feet with their long, tapered toes. Every moment he spent with Paula, it seemed to him, peeled back new, previously unexplored layers of perversion in his mind.

Pacing the room, he recounted, as his gramps and Brenda had given it to him, the tale of Rigby's assault the night before on a stranger in the Town Crier, a man whose only offense was calling him "faggot."

She wasn't much concerned. "He's done worse than that, believe me. Didn't he throw up on a girl the night he met you?"

It was late afternoon in the bungalow's living room, dust motes churning bright in the shaft of cool spring sun from above. "The provocation in this case was pretty mild," Keith said.

"Don't be a pussy, Keith."

"I'm not being a pussy. He beat a guy nearly unconscious."

"Don't exaggerate, then. Sometimes he takes things too seriously. Especially when it's a challenge to his manliness."

He was simultaneously aroused and made nervous by the painting of the toenails. He couldn't help picturing her husband, with his jacked-up musculature and what Keith now understood to be very poor impulse control, walking in and finding Keith watching Paula in this oddly intimate, though not explicitly sexual, situation, and casually twisting Keith's head clean off his shoulders like the cap on a soda bottle.

"Does he take steroids?" he asked.

"Don't be ridiculous, he didn't do that even when he was in competition. That's half the reason he quit, the sport was just overrun with juicers. This isn't giving you second thoughts, is it?" she said, never looking up from her task. She smelled good, too, as she always did, a subtle, floral fragrance that she seemed to give off naturally, too faint and subtle to have been produced by any mortal cosmetics manufacturer. He didn't think he was in love with her so much as hooked on her look and the sound and smell and touch.

She finished working on her toes and turned her face up toward his, coquettish and pouty. "How long until you have to be back at the club?"

"I only had one lesson this afternoon. I canceled it to come meet you."

"You lost money because you wanted to tell me how scared you were of my husband?" she asked with equal parts amusement and disdain. Then she lifted an eyebrow and pursed her lips. "That must make you awful mad, when I challenge your masculinity that way."

"Not really."

"No, I can tell it does. You must just want to push me back onto this couch and lift my ankles into the air and spank me bare-assed with that rolled-up copy of the *Times* there."

Following her gaze he saw that there was indeed a stack of unread papers, rolled and rubber-banded. As he advanced, wielding one menacingly in his right hand, she leaned back and lifted her knees to her chest.

"Spank me!" she said, voice low and breathy, and after the first blow, at which she let out a piteous whimper, she added, "Careful of my nails, if you get polish on this couch I'll kill you myself."

THE NEXT DAY, HE went over to his grandfather's house on Channel Drive. He found the old man in the garage out back, to which he'd added a skylight, converting it into a full-time, dedicated studio. "Close the door, boy, I don't want people watching me paint."

He did as he was told and admired the painting on the easel. A painting of a dark-haired, olive-skinned woman with a long, noble face and aquiline nose, she looked at the viewer with an expression of yearning.

"That's a good one. Who's she?"

"Just a gal I knew once."

"It doesn't look like your style."

"Used to be my style a long time ago."

"Why'd you change it?"

"I matured."

"It's a good picture," Keith said.

"You're repeating yourself."

He took a seat a few feet away and watched as his

grandfather soaked a clean rag in turpentine and applied it to the center of the canvas, first making the woman's nose glisten and then blur. He stood up and came closer, shocked at this desecration. "What are you doing that for? You're ruining it."

"I need the canvas. I'm saving your girlfriend Mrs. Rigby from foreclosure and ignominy."

"But the painting." The aristocratic face was gone except for her chin and a fragment of her extended lower lip and a good deal of her forehead.

"My old teacher, Vassily Kushik, had all his canvases stretched by the same stoop-shouldered old guy in Ojai, Alvin Doggner. I used Alvin when I was young, too, because I thought that's what you did. Only one of those canvases I have left is this one. I don't even know why I saved it. Hadn't looked at it in sixty years until yesterday."

"That's a shame, wasting a good painting like that."

"I'm going to paint a better one. But if the canvas wasn't right, we'd be found out the first time anyone looked at it."

"Isn't it going to some school that's not even going to know what they've got?"

"That's no excuse for doing a half-assed job, boy." His grandfather interrupted his obliteration of the woman's face. "I started thinking about it, realized I had it in me to do a great one. I mix my own oils, same as I did back then, the way old Kushik taught me, same way he did it. It occurred to me I could do one that was better than what they needed. I knew the old bastard's working methods better than anybody. If I can't fool the experts, nobody can."

He dipped the rag once more and went back to applying the turpentine. All that remained of the woman was a smear of dark brown hair and her dress, a mélange of reds and oranges that suggested a patterned silk and a bit of rosy arm.

"Now, what I'm doing here is getting the paint soft so I can wipe off the thickest of it. Later, when it's down to the texture of the canvas, I'll get rid of all the pigment, right down to the gesso. Once the gesso's off I'll put on a fresh coat, and I'll be ready to do Kushik's version of the old girl."

"Still, too bad you had to ruin the portrait. She was beautiful."

"Believe me, it was my pleasure."

CHAPTER TWENTY

BRITT WARDEN'S DEATH HAD cost the firm every single one of his clients, not a one of whom was willing to trust his business to Rigby. After six months, he'd been obliged to move the office to smaller and less distinguished quarters and reduce the firm's staff from five to one. The new space was downtown in what he'd been assured was once the tallest building in Ventura County. It had undeniable mid-century charm, with built-in walnut bookcases and a view of the Pacific across the 101. Damned few lawyers practiced downtown anymore, though, and every time he came into the office to be greeted without enthusiasm by his sole employee he was reminded of his diminished station, which called to mind in turn the other recent troubles occasioned by the decline in revenues. He wasn't terribly bothered today, though; everything was in line, and he'd have Glenn's money back in his account before the body was cold, or at least before the accountants got their hands on the books.

Four days had passed since he'd shot Billy Knox and his girlfriend. He stopped in at five o'clock to check on his mail, and he took immediate note of the pinched expression on Lena's face as he entered the tiny reception area. Neither of them said hello. "You look like you haven't taken a shit in a week," he said in passing.

She took a deep breath and pulled her chair back and drummed a staccato, four-knuckled tattoo on the desktop. "Okay, first off, we've been over this before, about your language. I'm your employee, and I object to being spoken to in that manner. You're an attorney, you should know better."

Oh, right—humorless bitch—he'd forgotten that about her since the day before yesterday. Jesus. "I'm very sorry, Lena." Between Lena and the priest and God, he was doing a lot more apologizing lately than was his custom or preference. "What else is the matter?"

"You haven't answered your cell all day." The way her mouth was set, it really did look as though she'd just guzzled a jar of vinegar. "It's one thing, you not being in here during business hours, but you have to be reachable. Mr. Haskill's nephew called four times from St. Louis. This is the fifth day he's called and I'm getting tired of it."

"Fuck," he muttered, quietly enough that Lena didn't feel obliged to object. "All right, get him for me, would you?"

He stepped back into the office and leaned back in his twelve-hundred-dollar chair, purchased shortly after he and Britt left the old firm and opened their own. Nervous Britt was against such cosmetic extravagances, but Rigby overruled him, saying they didn't want to look like a couple of kids right out of law school. That was the thing about that partnership, they'd really balanced out one another's weaknesses. He had no doubt whatsoever that if Britt hadn't gotten himself killed, he wouldn't be in anywhere near this kind of trouble. *Fucking dumb shit. Ice climbing, he might as well have jumped out of a goddamned airplane without a chute.*

"Mr. Rigby, I have Mr. Haskill on one."

He picked up the receiver with a sense of nonspecific dread. "Jerry, Rigby here. How the hell are you?"

"Oh, just fine. Just have a few questions about my uncle."

About your uncle's money, you mean, you bloodsucking prick.
The nephew stood to inherit in the low eight figures' worth of
cash and securities, plus the house, plus what remained
of the old man's television revenues, which thanks to the
insatiable programming demands of cable were still worth
some money. "Sure, go ahead."

"I ran into some people from my old high school. Uncle
Glenn's alma mater, too."

"Right."

"Anyway this guy, he's the director of development, he
says Uncle Glenn's going to make some sort of bequest to
the school. In his will."

"That's where a bequest normally goes, Jerry."

"Hah. I was just wondering what kind of bequest. What
size, actually."

In fact the amount in the will was $35,000, but Rigby liked
making the nephew squirm. "I'm not really free to discuss
such things, but your uncle can tell you if you're concerned."

"Oh."

Jerry wasn't ever going to bring this up with old Glenn.
He was so terrified of being disinherited he never brought
money up in the old man's presence, even though it came
up every single time he spoke to Rigby.

"This guy was also telling me something about a painting.
You know the one I'm talking about?"

Fuck. Fuck, fuck, fuck.

"Yeah. What about it?"

"Have you seen it?"

"I sure have." Now it struck him that if Jerry had ever seen
the picture they were screwed, because he would certainly
be present for its installation at the school.

"Is it really that special? I know he has a lot of pictures,
but as I remember they're all shit."

"Oh, I don't know that much about art, but the girl who works for him now, she's got a master's degree in art history and she says it's crap."

"The development guy says there was some article on this guy in a magazine. Sounds to me like it might be worth a lot of money. Maybe more than we want to give the school."

"Jerry, that's just your uncle fucking with them. You know how he feels about that place." *Don't say anything right now that's going to fuck up my beautiful scheme. Do not. Because I will reach in through the telephone wire and rip out your fucking trachea from two thousand fucking miles away.*

"So how concrete is the plan to give it to the school?"

"Nothing's official yet."

"Maybe we could keep it unofficial, and then when he's, you know, when he's gone we could figure it out then? We could sell it or maybe even give it to the school anyway if the spirit moves us."

Thank God. The dumb bastard was willing to let Rigby handle the talking himself. This wasn't a roadblock or even a major detour, then, just a slow-moving garbage truck that had to be passed on the wrong side. "I'll plant the idea in his head and see what comes up, all right? You take care of yourself now, Jerry."

He hung up and kept talking. "Yeah, take care of your pig-faced, sexless, ball-sucking bag of greedy shit self. You pale, stuttering, hairless pile of worthless human garbage. You worthless goat-fucking taste-like-assburger."

"I can hear you all the way out here, Mr. Rigby," Lena called from out in reception.

THREE HOURS LATER, LENA was long gone. Rigby sat alone in his darkened office, looking out at the cars passing on the freeway, dipping an occasional wet fingertip into a small baggie of coke that he kept in the locked top-right drawer of the desk. The predominant sensation in his brain was optimism; the worry clinging to him for the past few weeks had begun to wither and fall away.

He was well aware that the cocaine was contributing mightily to this feeling, but it hadn't had the same effect on him recently, had, in fact, been exacerbating his general antsiness. He'd been listening to KFI to see if there was anything about a grisly discovery in a Ventura County summer home, and surfing the local TV stations' websites looking for any sign someone had found the bodies. Nobody was looking, it seemed, for Knox or his girlfriend, and by the time they were found no one would be able to establish that Rigby had ever had anything to do with the runty little fuck. He was sure now that they weren't in that house for any legitimate reason—tweakers weren't renowned for their reliability as house sitters—at some point someone would stumble upon what was left of them, and the cops would tally up the contents of the house, including what Rigby assumed would be a small meth stash, and come to the entirely reasonable conclusion that someone in the drug trade had had it in for little Billy Knox.

Which of course was true, but Rigby knew that they wouldn't be looking for a more or less respectable attorney as the killer. Nor would they spend the effort necessary to come to such an unlikely conclusion regarding the deaths of the likes of those two.

And then his office line rang. He never picked up himself in the office, but he looked to see who it was. The caller ID was blocked, and the cocaine was telling him to pick up or he'd worry about it later.

"Mr. Rigby? This is Ernie Norwin."

Jesus, what now? "Sure. How you doing, Ernie?"

"Hope you don't mind me calling."

Fuck fuck fuck fuck. "That's fine, what's on your mind?"

"Just wondering if you'd seen Billy. His girlfriend Magda's mom keeps calling me, like she thinks I'm up to something because Magda was supposed to meet her in Chatsworth and she didn't show."

"Well, I'll be honest with you, Ern, Knox sure did fuck up that job I had him do, big time. And despite having fucked up said job beyond all recognition, he felt entitled to his payment."

"That's what he told me last time I saw him down at the Shanty. Said he was going to get that money out of you one way or the other."

"He got some of it. Beat me up pretty good."

Norwin was quiet for a moment. "Billy Knox did?"

"Snuck up on me with a tire iron. Took everything I had on me, and I was carrying over three thousand in cash for a client, supposed to make a bank deposit the next morning. Had to make it up out of my own pocket."

"Huh. I didn't think he had the balls."

"I imagine he bought some dope and they hightailed it off somewhere to sell it, or else just snort it up. You talk to anyone else about this?"

"No," Norwin said, slowly, and Rigby could almost hear the gears turning just as painfully inside the man's head on the other end. "Why's that?"

"See, I could get into trouble if it got out that I'd lost a client's money."

"You said you paid it back yourself."

"Yeah, but there are rules about how to do these things, and I didn't follow them. Also it's not good press that I got beaten up by a guy over a debt. A crooked one at that."

By the time the call ended Norwin sounded as though he

believed that Knox and Magda just ran off somewhere on a tear, and the electrical feeling in Rigby's belly had subsided to a tolerable degree, but the fact remained that Norwin knew there was a serious conflict between him and the dead man. That would have to be dealt with before any discoveries were made.

From the locked drawer he retrieved the phone he took off Knox. He checked the call log on the office phone and punched Norwin's number into the burner.

ITS ME BILLY

He hesitated before pressing SEND, since there was now a telephone record somewhere of Norwin having called him that very evening, a record of their existences having intersected, but the moment seemed to call for bold action.

Dude where you been mags moms going nuts she didn't show up chatswrth

WERE HOLED UP WANT A TASTE?

sure where you at

Rigby grinned, feeling lucky, and calculated how long it was going to take him to get out to the Ojai house, then started typing directions.

CHAPTER TWENTY-ONE

IT HAD BEEN ODD getting into the rhythms of aping Kushik again, something he'd worked hard to get out of while he was studying with the man himself. The maestro had started mocking him at one point back in the day for his slavish imitation of his own style, and now Will understood that part of the problem was his very facility; it couldn't have been easy to watch even an eager acolyte matching your style stroke by stroke, getting close to the point of bettering it. So he'd veered away, but not too far, and developed a style that was in the vein of Kushik without being mistakable for the genuine article. And then, after the disaster with Judy, he'd rejected the entire school and done an about-face, shitcanning all that palette-knife heavy impasto and brushy, sketchy pseudo-impressionist bullshit. It was a pleasure to realize, after a few days of sketching and daubing at canvases and wiping them clean and starting over, that he still had Kushik's style in his muscle memory. He was surprised to discover that he liked doing it again, that there was still a visceral pleasure in being able to paint in the old man's style.

He had Keith drive him up to the art museum in Santa Barbara. It held at least three Kushiks, according to the Internet, and he remembered watching two of them come into being in the Ojai studio. Seeing them on the Internet wasn't enough, though, he needed to look at them close-up and in person.

To his credit, the boy didn't complain about taking the day off to serve as his chauffeur. He had never shown much interest in art, apart from feigning a polite appreciation of his grandfather's work.

"So is that the same lady?" he said. They were heading northward on State Street, not far from the museum.

"What lady?" The boy had a way of assuming that you were privy to the conversation going on silently in his head.

"The lady you're drawing. Is she the lady in the painting you wiped clean?"

"She is. Keep it quiet, all right?"

"Okay. Why?"

"Because I asked you to, all right?" Jesus. The kid hadn't changed since he was five years old and every other word out of his mouth was "why." But at least he was good enough to drive his grandfather around when asked.

HE WALKED INTO THE museum with trepidation. He was overreaching, surely, imagining that he could convincingly fake as well-documented an artist as Kushik. But he took solace from the sure knowledge that by the time his fraud was discovered, he'd be dead and unpunishable.

He'd been to the museum on a number of occasions but had scrupulously avoided the Kushiks. They hung side by side on their own wall in a large gallery space. The first was a still life of drying chili peppers, the second an unfamiliar seascape with characteristically overdramatic cliffs and sky. The third was a portrait of a little girl Will had sketched during the same sitting. He remembered her well, though his sketches were long gone. A solemn child of eight or nine with serious black eyes, she'd asked questions during the sitting that Kushik actually deigned to answer. Usually he shushed sitters with such vehemence they didn't dare speak again until dismissed at the end of a session, but he'd seemed impressed with the girl's gravitas. Will wondered what had become of the child. The plaque beside the painting read "Portrait of a Chumash Girl."

Staring at the paintings one by one he studied the familiar brushwork, the bold slashes and wily curves and showy building-up of one tone over another; he was overwhelmed with a strong sense of having been long ago deceived. He felt crestfallen and elated in equal amounts. Kushik's style was all bravura and showy technique, and whatever he'd once admired in these paintings failed to conjure itself now. The tastes of Russian billionaires notwithstanding, these were valuable paintings without being especially great ones, and the moderate success Kushik had enjoyed during his life-time had been more than he'd deserved. Will's fear of his own hubris disappeared, replaced by the sure knowledge that he could not only convincingly duplicate a Kushik, he could do a better one than the man himself ever did. His revenge would come in the form of enhancing the old bas-tard's reputation undeservedly. No one who'd ever known the man in life would know about it besides Will Seghers, and that was oddly part of the sweetness of it.

CHAPTER TWENTY-TWO

HASKILL HADN'T CALLED DOWN for his breakfast by the usual time, so at nine-thirty she went up with the tray and found him sitting up in bed looking at the wall.

"Mr. Haskill, I have your breakfast."

He turned and a string of drool swung along with his chin. Meeting her gaze, he betrayed no sign of recognition and she put the tray down.

"Oh, shit."

His skin was ashy and cool to the touch, and she helped him back to a reclining position before calling 911. Then she called Rigby.

"Mr. Haskill's feeling very poorly this morning. The ambulance is on the way and you'd better get here, too." The old man was watching her, puzzled, and when she hung up he put his head down onto the pillow and let loose a loud sigh.

"I just don't seem to have my usual get-up-and-go," he said, closed his eyes and immediately began snoring.

SHE WAS IN THE kitchen with Rigby drinking coffee while the EMTs and his personal physician examined Haskill upstairs. "You need to put the painting somewhere safe."

"This house is safe as anywhere in California. You know what the old coot spends on security a month?"

"If this is the end of the line, the nephew will be coming out. He can't see the picture."

"He doesn't know which picture it is."

"He's bound to want to see it, and once he's seen it we can't give the fake to the school."

Rigby nodded. "Okay. I'll rent a safe-deposit box."

"Just stash it in your office. You can tell him it's in the bank."

"You think this really is the end?"

"You should have seen him. Like Nosferatu with a pencil mustache."

Dr. Pulliver came down with the EMTs, Haskill supine on a folding gurney. At the bottom of the stairs, they extended the legs and wheeled him out to the waiting ambulance.

"So what's he got?"

The doctor pursed his lips and looked at the ceiling, and Nina had the distinct impression that he didn't have any idea what was ailing Haskill. "He's a very old man with multiple serious health conditions and they're just catching up with him now. I'll be honest, when I see a decline this rapid, I get a terrible feeling," the doctor said. "You'd better call the nephew and tell him to come see him."

"You're the doctor," she said. This clown had been Haskill's doctor since the eighties, and the only thing Nina could see he had going for him was his willingness to make house calls to rich patients.

After Pulliver left, they went upstairs and Nina wrapped the Kushik in clear plastic, then placed it carefully in a suitcase filled with towels.

"I'll take this to the office as soon as I'm done at the hospital," Rigby said.

"Forget the hospital, take it to the office right now, or your house, or wherever. The old man's not going anywhere."

THE NEXT AFTERNOON ANOTHER ambulance brought Haskill home, and once the attendants had managed to get him up to the bedroom where the first shift nurse awaited, Dr. Pulliver explained to her and Rigby the rules of the house.

"He's not to be left alone for any length of time. If the nurse registers any decline, she or he will call for you on the intercom, and you'll call me and then him," he said, pointing at Rigby.

The various and sundry tests performed at the hospital had revealed no new conditions, just a general worsening of the old ones. Maybe the doctor had been right. In any case he wasn't talking much, which was the most alarming difference, and he showed no interest in anyone's presence. The only thing he said to her that night when she spelled the nurse for a fifteen-minute break was that he wanted the needle out of his arm.

"That's your IV, Mr. Haskill, it's keeping you alive."

"I don't want it," he said. "Who the hell are you, anyway?"

CHAPTER TWENTY-THREE

"YOU SURE ARE PAINTING fast," his grandson said.

"Don't you have any lessons this afternoon?"

"Am I bothering you?"

"Not really."

He was working fast, the way Kushik used to, the way he used to himself. It had been the one thing he'd been uncertain about before starting, because he'd adopted a much slower, more natural pace for himself in the intervening years. It was the only way to do it right, though, and he was pleased to find that he could still do it. The picture appearing bit by bit before him looked like Kushik's work, right down to the pissed-off-looking impasto on the fringes.

"You have any pictures of this lady to go by?"

"Not a one. Apart from the painting I wiped off of this canvas, I haven't laid eyes on her or any image thereof in more than sixty years."

"You have a better memory than I do."

"It's funny, I could go years without being able to picture her in my mind's eye. Just a vague image of a brunette, medium height, willowy. I could picture a dress she used to wear, but the face was a blur. Then out of the blue I'd see her as though she were standing in front of me."

Maybe it came from looking at his old painting of her, or maybe it was the act of imagining how Kushik would have painted her. In any case the woman he was reconstructing on the canvas was the woman he'd known, right down to the melancholy in her gray eyes. She didn't always look that way, but that was the expression he remembered most vividly. He had always guessed it had to do with her kids, stuck incommunicado in Maine with her estranged and vengeful husband, but she'd never put it into words, not to him.

"So how come you stopped talking to her?"

"You ask a lot of questions."

"Sorry. You want me to go?"

"No, stick around. Kushik was always holding forth while he painted, it helps with the process."

"So how come?"

He took a long, deep breath. "I took the thing way too seriously. She was a married woman, on the run, decided she wanted to paint. She was good, too, and in those days it took a certain amount of gumption to want to do serious figurative painting. So we were both in Kushik's circle, and he didn't take on that many acolytes. It was just a friendly working relationship until one day she asked if I wanted to drive to Colorado, rent a cabin down by the Rio Grande. So we went, spent ten days painting and playing house and then we drove back."

"Was that near where we went that one time, where the guy killed the guy who killed the other guy?"

"That's it, these tourist cabins were just down the road from Creede. Little Bob Ford, who shot Jesse James, set up a saloon there, and a man named O'Kelley shot him dead."

"So that's why you took us there?"

"I liked the area. Good fishing, pretty little town."

"And nostalgia for the lady?"

"I don't think so. I developed my own relationship to the place. But it's true that the first time I went was with her."

"So what happened when you went back?"

"I didn't behave very well, I suppose. She'd made it plain from the outset that it was just for fun and nothing serious, she was already married, and anyway, I was just a kid of twenty-six or -seven."

"I can't help thinking twenty-six or -seven wasn't such a kid back then, especially after the war."

"Yeah, I bristled at that, having fought a world war and traveled the world as widely as possible in that pre-jetliner era, but then I proved her point by storming off and acting like a petulant boy when she ended it."

"So she left you for the teacher."

"No, that came later. But that was the last straw with me and Kushik. I'd been wanting to go my own way for a while, so it was a good excuse."

"How much longer before you're done with it?"

"Damn near finished right now. The old man always used to say quit before you're quite done, it's better to underwork a picture than overwork it." He got off the stool and stepped back. After thirty seconds he changed brushes. "Glad you brought that up. Seems to me this is as good a stopping point as any. And here's the most important part."

He added a large jaunty slash of a K to the lower-right-hand corner.

"And now to let it dry. Tomorrow I can start the aging process, two, three days after that it'll be ready to go."

He covered it with a canvas drop cloth and they left the studio.

IN THE KITCHEN HE poured himself and the boy iced tea from the pitcher he kept in the fridge. "So are you still mad about her and Kushik?"

"I was wondering that myself. Until I needed that canvas,

I hadn't thought about it in a long time, and I guess I don't feel much at all. Maybe it was just her unsuitability that had made her so attractive. If she'd been single and my own age and eager to marry me, I might have kept her at arm's length the way I did any number of other girls."

"Huh. Maybe it's something I get from you, then."

"Maybe so. I don't approve, exactly, but I do understand your urge to transgress."

They stepped out the back door and sat down on the brick kitchen steps and looked out onto the old flower garden. "Begonias are looking sickly, aren't they?" he said.

The boy squinted. "Which ones are they?"

"Long leaves, little white flowers in a bunch there. Too goddamn hot this spring. Not even the end of May and it's like this."

"Speaking of the heat, you smell something?"

He took a deep sniff and nodded. "Now you mention it, I've been half-processing something in my olfactory lobe for a day or two. But it's definitely there now." He set down his iced tea and approached the garden. Behind the begonias and against the fence to the neighbor's yard lay an enormous dead raccoon, several days gone.

CHAPTER TWENTY-FOUR

IT HAD BEEN THREE days since the assistant, what's-her-name, had called to inform him of Uncle Glenn's steep and sudden decline. The cost of flying the next day would have been ruinous, and he'd been too embarrassed to ask for the airfare, although the woman had cautioned him that Uncle Glenn might not last more than a day or two. With a bit of digging on the Web, he discovered that he could save over five hundred dollars by waiting three days and flying out of Kansas City, even factoring in the price of gas and a night in a hotel. The airport was four hours' distance from home if you did eighty the whole time, and at 5 P.M., he was almost at the halfway point. He pulled off at the Auxvasse/Mexico exit for gas.

He'd forgotten to eat lunch, and once he'd filled up, he went into the C store and picked a sandwich out of a cooler, ham and American cheese with mayo, sliced diagonally and preserved for the ages in cling wrap. He ate it sitting in the parking lot and called on long-dormant fifth-grade math skills to calculate the Cutlass's mileage per gallon. After several false starts, he was pretty certain he'd nailed it at nearly thirty MPG, which impressed him; despite its lack of modern amenities, like satellite radio, the twenty-year-old Cutlass was turning out to be quite a satisfactory vehicle. He made a plan to buy his mother a better car to replace it once he was rich again, maybe one of those Caddies that zigged.

He'd managed to get a four-and-a-half star hotel room for seventy dollars and change. The only drawback was its location: the Kansas City airport was miles from downtown and anything you might want to do of an evening. It was seven-thirty when he arrived, and after a shower and a change of clothes, he crossed the hotel parking lot to the adjacent Outback Steakhouse, where he ordered a pork porterhouse and a twenty-ounce Foster's lager in a chilled glass rimmed with frost that gave him a violent twenty-second headache.

Afterward he stopped in the hotel's lobby bar. The only other customer was a man in a blue suit with his tie loosened, presumably to make room for a double chin worthy of a bullfrog. The bartender, a small woman with cat-eye glasses and close-cropped magenta hair, took his order without enthusiasm, then returned her attention to the Royals game on the set over the bar.

Jerry more or less followed the game out of a need for something to occupy his mind until a tall blond woman sat down a couple of stools to his right.

"Hi, Vickie," the bartender said, brightening considerably. "Where you in from?"

"Los Angeles."

"Ooh."

"Yeah, outside LA, actually, so twice as much driving."

"Yuck. Well, welcome to KC."

"Ronny been around lately?"

"Just last week, he asked after you."

He listened to their conversation, eyes on the television. After a couple of minutes, the man in the blue suit hailed the bartender, and while she tended to him, Jerry turned to the woman. "Did I hear you say you were just in LA? I'm heading there tomorrow. Santa Barbara."

"Not the same thing. Nice up there, though."

"I'm going to say goodbye to my uncle. He's on his deathbed."

"Are you close to him?"

He hesitated, and then to his own surprise found his eyes welling. "I am," he said.

"Sorry. Hakuna matata, though, right?"

"Sorry, what was that?"

The woman smiled. She was about his age, he guessed, and had excellent, straight teeth. "You never had kids, I take it."

He shook his head, feeling as if she were passing judgment on him. "No."

"Well, sorry about your uncle."

"What brought you to California?"

"I'm an attorney for a chain of storage facilities, we had a client die in one of the units out in West Covina. You know it?"

"No."

"It's a shithole. Out east of town, kind of in the direction of San Berdoo and Ontario and the desert."

"Ontario, that's where I'm flying into."

"To get to Santa Barbara? That's original, I guess."

The bartender had returned and was following the conversation without speaking. "Tricia, listen to this. So I get called out to LA because we had a tenant die in one of the units. This guy signs in one afternoon and hasn't signed out by closing time, so the manager on duty goes to check on him. Did I mention this guy's in arrears by about a grand? Anyway, manager opens the unit, finds the guy dead with a belt around his throat attached to the rack the door slides open on."

"What?" the bartender said.

"And all around him on the floor is porno. Now I'm pretty open-minded, but the sheriff showed me and this is, like, bathroom stuff, you know? Sheriff says it's autoerotic asphyxiation, guy was jerking off and choking himself with the belt and when the moment came he passed out and never woke up. Can you top that?"

Jerry couldn't remember any woman ever talking to him like this, not just about sex but about perversion.

"So why'd they need you out there?"

"So the widow denies he even had a storage unit and wants to sue. So it's been in the paper that he died, but not that he hanged himself with his dick in his hand in a storage unit with some of the most disturbing images ever printed lying on the ground in front of him."

"Could they even put that in the paper?" Jerry said.

"Who knows, but I told her lawyer we'd countersue for his back rent, and I made sure to point out how interested the newspapers would be in the whole business."

"That's cold, Vickie."

"So we comp his back rent and their lawyer backs down, and the manager cleans the unit out. And it's all porno. All of it."

He tried to think of something clever to say, something that would sound worldly and sophisticated, something that might make this Vickie find him interesting, but nothing came to him.

"Got an early flight tomorrow," he said, and got no reaction from either woman. "Can I get another Bushmills to take to my room?"

CHAPTER TWENTY-FIVE

THE TRAFFIC INTO VENTURA County from LAX was hellish, made more so by the fact that Freyda Wilkins refused to shut the fuck up despite the fact that neither Vanessa nor Cressida had responded to a single of her utterances for the past twenty-five minutes. Vanessa felt bad about this, because it was good of Freyda to come and pick them up, but all she could think was, *Sweet bleeding Jesus Christ, just please pick up on the vibe from your passengers and shut your cakehole.* Currently, Freyda was nattering on about some arcane difficulty her oldest son Steiner was having getting his acupressure clinic licensed in Salt Lake City. Vanessa countered a powerful urge to suggest that Steiner move his acupressure business someplace more New Agey than Salt Lake City. The boy had rebelled in his early twenties in a manner perfectly consistent with having been raised among hippie lesbians in Ojai by meeting a Mormon girl, converting, marrying her and moving to Utah. This union, though troubling, had thus far blessed Freyda with five grandchildren, with another on the way and probably many more after that. Vanessa had never asked what the Mormon in-laws thought of Freyda's living arrangements, though she suspected it was one of those things that simply wasn't brought up. Grandma had a roommate who was like one of the family, was how they probably explained it to the grandkids.

In the backseat, Cressida scowled out the window at the passing scenery, and Vanessa was grateful for the kind of repressed rage that occasionally brought her to bitter silence, because this would otherwise have been the occasion for an epic rant: multi-car pileup at Trancas leading to a miles-long backup; Subaru minivan dating back to the era before Japanese manufacturers got wise to the fact that American consumers wanted their air conditioners spewing temperatures suited to the farthest, iciest reaches of the solar system; sweet, ditsy Freyda, unable to judge the degree of interest among her passengers in her son's professional dramas; finally, the CD changer fully loaded with Enya. All of it could have been avoided by turning on KFI and getting the traffic report, but the potent, relaxing sounds of Enya prevailed.

Finally Vanessa realized she couldn't take another second of the tale of poor Steiner and she blurted out the question she'd been avoiding. "So what's the word on Magda?"

"Oh, Lordy, poor Cheyenne, she's just beside herself. She's pretty sure it's the sleazeball boyfriend, the sheriff's department thinks so too, turns out he's into drugs, well, we knew that, didn't we? But not just using, apparently selling, is what the rumor on the street is, and no one's seen hide nor hair of him, which is normal, but Magda? She's nothing if not reliable at work. In fact, it was that vet she works for who called Cheyenne to tell her something was wrong because Magda, when she's sick she'll just show up anyway. They've had to send her home before when she's had the flu for fear she'd give it to the people bringing their pets in! So when she missed two days in a row without phoning, well, that seemed funny."

"I didn't know about the boyfriend."

"Uneducated and uncultured, Cheyenne says, no

inclination to work—the only good thing is they aren't living together. For the life of me, a smart, strong-willed girl like her, how she gets involved with a creep like that."

"Maybe he's got a sweet side," Vanessa said.

"Maybe he's hung like a rhinoceros," Cressida said from the backseat, and in the rearview Vanessa could see a nasty smirk on her face, a welcome sign that her mood was improving.

"WHAT ARE THOSE CARS doing here?" Cressida asked when they pulled into the long gravel drive.

They were meant to return in January, but Vanessa broke her hip and required four months' convalescing and rehab at a facility in St. Pete's. Cressida had wanted to call the housecleaning service before they arrived, but Vanessa pointed out that, since the house was spotless upon their departure in November, the only cleanup required would be dusting.

"I have no idea," Vanessa said. A dilapidated pickup truck and a faded Buick Century were parked at the front door, the driver's-side door of the pickup standing open.

Vanessa's hip was hurting after the flight and the drive and she limped toward the front door with her carry-on while Cressida and Freyda wrestled with the larger baggage. She peered into the truck's cab and noted that the dome light wasn't illuminated. The door-open beeper wasn't going off, either.

A good ten feet from the door she became aware of a powerful and disagreeable odor emanating from the interior. "Uh-oh, Cress, I think we might have a dead possum." The closer she got the more intense the smell became, and by the time she had her key out she had to pull a scarf from her bag and hold it in front of her face.

"Shit, I can smell it all the way back here," Cressida said, suitcase handles in both hands.

"You really should be careful to empty the house of food before you leave town," Freyda said, and only the fact that she was hauling one of Vanessa's suitcases kept Vanessa from making a remark that might wipe that superior look off her face.

Cressida and Freyda were standing behind her holding the bags as Vanessa unlocked the top bolt and then the knob, and when she pushed the door inward an outrush of icy, fetid, malodorous gas rushed over her face, and she dropped on her knees to the gravel. A cloud of flies of varying colors and sizes poured from the crack between door and frame, and as one buzzed briefly, alarmingly, into her open mouth, she spat and choked and, finally, puked. The swarm brushed her face, landing on her hair and arms, pausing as if to consider her suitability as a site for feeding or the laying of eggs before moving on to more promising possibilities, and in the near distance she heard Cressida and Freyda scream.

CHAPTER TWENTY-SIX

THE EVENING NURSE HAD arrived at six, and hadn't bothered hiding her shock at Haskill's deterioration. Nina had heard her conferring with the second-shift nurse—there were three full-time shifts now—estimating the time he had left. They were in disagreement about what was going to kill him first, but they agreed the time was at hand. A week, two at the outside.

Off the clock now, she was driving down to Ventura for her first look at Will's finished painting. If it passed inspection, they were set and ready to move as soon as Glenn Haskill drew his last wheezy breath. In any case, she was confident that it would be good enough to fool whoever needed to be fooled back in Missouri.

She parked in front of Will's house and went around back to the garage studio, where she found him in conversation with a man about her own age dressed in golf clothes.

"Nina, this is my grandson Keith. Keith, Nina. She's here to look at the picture."

Nina said nothing, but accepted the younger man's proffered hand.

"Nice to meet you," he said.

"Nina, you mind if the two of us move that clock before we get started? Won't take long."

A big grandfather clock stood in a corner of the studio,

where according to Will it had done for thirty-five or more years, and on her previous visit here, she'd pointed out to him that it was a Sheraton-style piece, made of mahogany and surely worth thousands of dollars. Haskill's misapprehensions about the value of his goods were one thing; he was a vulgarian and too rich to worry about the precise value of a painting. But Will Seghers was a man of taste without great means, and she wondered how he could see a clock like that and not sense that it had monetary worth.

"I can do it myself," the boy said. "I brought the hand truck."

"All right, then, if you're sure you don't want a hand." He watched his grandson tip the top of the clock backward and slide the lip of the hand truck underneath it, then slowly roll it out of the garage and toward the house.

"Boy sometimes seems like he doesn't know how much a whole bunch of nines is, but he's got a good practical intelligence."

"I think you should be more careful about who has access to this garage," Nina said.

"He knows all about this already. He's the one put me and Rigby together in the first place."

"The more people who know about it, the more risk of someone talking."

"He's my grandson, he's not going to do anything to get me into trouble."

"No, but me? Rigby? If he was turning state's evidence to protect you?"

"Girly, I'm ninety-three years old. No prosecutor's going after me, and if they do, I'll croak a long time before they get me convicted."

Will got up and removed the drop cloth from the canvas, which caught the last bit of sunlight coming in through the west skylight. She took in a sharp breath at the sight of it, at its apparent age and its brutal fidelity to Kushik's style.

"Jesus, it's beautiful."

Will shrugged, and his indifference to her opinion seemed genuine. "Good enough for government work."

"No, it's fantastic. It's better than the real one."

Will grunted, something close to a chuckle. "Want to hear a story? Right after the war, I was on leave. I wanted to see a landscape by a Dutch painter by the name of Hercules Seghers."

"Relative of ours?" the grandson asked.

"Who can say. I wanted him to be. I liked the idea that art was something that flowed through my veins. Horseshit, but I was a young man. Anyway, this picture was in the Boijmans Museum in Rotterdam. So you can imagine how hard it was getting across Europe by train in early '46. Didn't have any Eurail passes in those days. But me and my buddy Marvin Buckner—we called him Bucky Fucknuts, pardon my language—we managed to get onto a train bound for Rotterdam. Bucky didn't give a damn about art, but he'd heard Dutch girls were easy."

"Were they?" the grandson asked.

"Not in my experience. Anyway, there in the main hall, there was this huge canvas, hanging from a freestanding wall in the center of the room. Jesus breaking bread with two women and a man. I stood there in front of it, just drank it in. And then Bucky Fucknuts sidles up next to me. He manages to keep his mouth shut for all of fifteen seconds before he says, 'So what's this one called, "Ugly Jesus?"' And I turned on him. I said, 'That happens to be a Vermeer, you ignorant son of a bitch, one of the greatest painters in the history of art.'

"And Bucky came back with 'He's kind of ugly's all I'm

saying.' And I said, 'Ugly's in the eye of the beholder, and if you know what's good for you you'll shut your hole till we leave the museum and I won't have to split your lip.'"

"Did he?" Nina said.

"He was easily cowed, Bucky was. So you've got a background in art history, Nina. You know where I'm going with this."

"A Vermeer in '46? I've got an idea."

He turned to his grandson. "This masterpiece I loved so much was a fake. They found the guy out a few months after I saw it. This son of a bitch painted a whole stack of the things. When the krauts invaded Holland, he started selling 'em to the Nazi brass. He was tried as a collaborator after the war for selling national treasures to the enemy. Nobody would believe he'd faked them all himself, he had to paint one in his cell to prove he was a forger and not a traitor."

The grandson nodded. "So what's the point of the story?"

"Point is, it doesn't have to be perfect if people want to believe."

Nina drew closer to inspect the surface. "This looks just about perfect to me. The craquelure looks right. How'd you get it?"

"Trade secret. Only way they'll prove that paint isn't as old as the canvas is a carbon-fourteen test."

She squinted at the woman on the canvas. "Is that Judith? The widow?"

"Judy's what I knew her by."

"She looks kind of scared."

"Take a look at any of Kushik's pictures of his mistresses and wives. They all look like they're scared they're going to say something wrong and spark that old Slavic temper."

"There isn't a real one of her. A real portrait, at least not one that survived."

"I never knew him to paint her. She was a painter herself, didn't let me paint her either. I had to do mine on the sly."

She studied it for a minute longer, and she thought Will was pleased with himself despite the feigned insouciance. "You know, a portrait of his last wife would probably be worth more than the real one."

SHE WAS ABOUT TO start her car and considering this possibility when her phone rang. She noted the caller's name with considerable dismay: JERRY HASKILL.

CHAPTER TWENTY-SEVEN

THE DEPUTY WATCHED FROM her cruiser as a compact, blond EMT with a teased hairdo straight out of 1987 tended to Mrs. Wilkins, who was seated on an Adirondack chair so weathered the deputy winced at the thought of sitting on it and getting splinters in her ass. Mrs. Wilkins's friends, Mrs. Hamner and Mrs. Backlin, had accepted the scene at their home with greater equanimity, and now that it seemed clear that Mrs. Wilkins was not in fact having a heart attack they were ready to make their statements.

Mrs. Hamner, the more dour of the two, went first, seated in the back of the cruiser. "Magda house-sat for us twice, when we still had cats and a dog, a big Newfoundland mix named Baxter we couldn't leave at the kennel because he'd refuse to eat. I don't know if that's a Newfie thing, he was a great dog otherwise."

"Where's the dog right now?"

Mrs. Hamner looked startled. "What's that got to do with it?"

"I assumed the dog had some relevance."

"He's dead. This was several years ago. The cats, too, we stopped replacing them when they died so we didn't need a house sitter anymore. I guess Magda must have kept the keys."

"We haven't established that the dead woman is Magda Schuller."

Mrs. Hamner leaned back and stared at her in the rear-view, and the deputy guessed she was a retired schoolteacher. Maybe a principal. "If not Magda, who is she, then?"

"We haven't established the dead woman's identity yet." She snapped it, mostly in frustration with herself; this was no way to take a statement. "How long has the house stood empty?"

"We've been gone since last fall. I suppose Magda and her scummy boyfriend might have been coming in on a regular basis, which really would have been fine—her mother's a dear friend of ours. I'm told Magda was living in a horrid little apartment in Moorpark, probably just wanted a nice place to relax in occasionally."

"And you got back tonight?"

"Around six. Freyda picked us up at LAX at four and took the slow route up. Did you hear about the wreck at Trancas this afternoon? Freyda didn't, and it cost us at least an hour."

"Ma'am, if you could stick to the subject at hand, we'll be done a lot quicker."

"I'm just trying to give you some context."

"When's the last time you spoke to Ms. Schuller?"

"I suppose it's been a couple of years. She didn't spend much time in Ojai anymore, not since she took up with that junkie scum."

"Wait, he was a junkie?"

"Oh, he was always knocked up with that methamphetamine, according to Cheyenne."

"That's a tweaker, Mrs. Hamner, not a junkie."

"I'm seventy-one years old, forgive me not being fully up-to-date on my narcotics slang. Anyway after she got together with Mr. Wonderful, she and Cheyenne had a few fairly bitter rows about her prospects for the future."

"Cheyenne is her mother?"

"Haven't you met her? I thought this was a big missing persons case."

"I don't work missing persons cases. The officer on that case is contacting Mrs. Schuller right now."

"It's not Schuller, that was her ex-husband's name. It's Cheyenne Burning Tree."

"And Ms. Burning Tree is Native American?"

Mrs. Hamner hesitated. "Let's say she self-identifies as such."

"Do you and Mrs. Backlin have a place to stay tonight?"

"I hadn't thought about it. I don't suppose we can stay here, can we?"

"Not while it's an active crime scene. After that you can do as you please, but in my experience, you're going to want to hire a crime scene cleanup outfit. That place is going to have a powerful odor sticking to it for a long time if you don't, and even if you do, you'll find yourself catching the odd whiff of it when you least expect it for months. I can give you a phone number if you like."

Mrs. Hamner got out of the cruiser to fetch Mrs. Backlin, standing next to Mrs. Wilkins in the Adirondack chair. The deputy was certain she'd get nothing useful from any of the three, but she'd rather be taking their statements than processing evidence in the house. Of all the crime scenes she'd ever worked, this was the foulest-smelling by far, three corpses roughly two and a half weeks dead, going by the date the Schuller woman went missing. Of course the dead woman was Magda Schuller, and one of the dead males was almost certainly Billy Knox, to whom the piece-of-shit pickup parked by the door was registered. One of the two men had been dead a considerably shorter amount of time than the other corpses, and his wound appeared to be self-inflicted. A trio of low-lifes, one of whom had ties to elderly bourgeois Ojai hippiedom and thus would rate a column inch or two in the Ventura County edition of the *L.A. Times*, snuffed out in some kind of shady crank deal gone south in a squat: not exactly the kind of case to waste a lot of man-hours on. The lab tech on the scene pointed out that the first two bodies had deteriorated in a manner consistent with very high temperatures like those experienced, unseasonably, in mid-May. Deceased White Male Number Two showed considerably less of what the ME would expect from such exposure, and when the women entered the house, the air conditioner was cranked up full blast. The way she saw it, DWM Number Two killed Knox and Schuller over some crank or some money and then came back to the house, got high and started feeling guilty and blew his brains out, but before he did it he cooled the house down. Why? Out of consideration for the owners? Or perhaps out of disgust at the condition of his victims, and possessed of a fear of his own decay. The deputy had been a psychology major before switching to administration of justice, and she maintained a strong interest in the field; what a fascinating case study this would have been, had the victims and the perpetrator been worthy of the law's full scrutiny.

UNLESS DWM NUMBER TWO turned out to be Knox. In that case, Knox must have found Magda and Deceased White Male Number One together and shot them out of jealousy—the Schuller woman's state of undress supported this scenario—then returned and in a druggy state of remorse shot himself. It was ugly but easy, and once these nice ladies got their house all cleaned up and smelling normal again no one would give a shit whether any of these jokers had ever existed or not.

CHAPTER TWENTY-EIGHT

BILLY KNOX HAD MADE the cable news cycle. It would be more accurate to say that his girlfriend Magda had, but Billy had managed to piggyback on her notoriety, as had Ventura County and environs.

"Ooh, look, Ventura," Beth said, taking a long slurp of her coffee. Rigby looked up to see a photo of Magda on the TV, above a title reading, FRIEND, BOYFRIEND OF MISSING CA WOMAN ALSO DEAD IN MURDER-SUICIDE, SAYS SHERIFF. In the photo, smiling sweetly and wearing pale blue scrubs, she looked much fresher than on the occasion of their sole meeting.

"Oh, my God, I know her, she works for Scruffy's vet," Beth said, her voice rising in pitch.

"Very pretty girl." That didn't jibe with his memory of that night, and he wondered how old the picture was.

"She's so nice! What do you think happened?"

"Five'll get you ten the boyfriend did it," Rigby said as Knox's photo replaced Magda's on-screen next to Ernie's, both photos betraying their seediness and addiction as much as Magda's had seemed to show her innocence and promise. For just an instant he caught himself believing that Knox had done her in, and when the truth shouldered itself into his consciousness, he was pleased at the extent to which that particular narrative rang true. Eventually a different one would come to light, slightly more complicated but, he hoped, equally compelling and credible. And then the anchor was back to talking about a deadly atrocity in the Middle East, and they turned their attention back to their scrambled eggs, bacon and cantaloupe. Rigby had wanted to go downstairs to the free breakfast buffet, but Beth was petrified at the thought of their crossing paths with someone from Ventura one or both of them knew, and no amount of logical persuasion could dissuade her. The night before, they'd taken in, at Beth's insistence, the Blue Man Group's show, following that with three hours of slot play, alcohol consumption and public displays of lust, but somehow in the morning light the threat of exposure took on new and more frightening dimensions for her. He had pointed out that in all the years he'd been coming to Vegas, he had never once run into anyone he knew from Ventura, but it was no good. She wouldn't so much as cross the lobby with him.

Vegas would have been a good place to find a priest and confess, if it was just to adultery and not murder. The priests there must have heard some truly gnarly shit over the years. He would have to consider very seriously whether or not he was going to take Communion the next Sunday. Surely Paula would notice a third Sunday in a row where he didn't, but he still hadn't worked out a confession strategy. What if the priest told him he had to turn himself in in order to be absolved? Could a priest do that? He wished he'd paid more attention in catechism class all those years ago. Paula would know, but he couldn't ask her, couldn't in fact ask anyone without looking guilty. And surely a DA would have a field day with a record of a Google search reading, CAN A PRIEST REQUIRE A MURDERER TO TURN HIMSELF IN AS PENANCE?

Paula *would* know, damn it. He took it as seriously as she

did, but not having been born into it meant he'd forgotten a lot of what he'd picked up during his instruction. Sometimes it was like trying to remember something from a contracts class he'd taken twenty years ago, vaguely familiar but if it was something he was going to wager his reputation on he'd want to go back and check the textbook. Britt hadn't been that way, he used to carry all of it in his head, and he could spout off statutes and quote decisions verbatim. It impressed the hell out of clients and judges alike, though Rigby had thought of it as little more than a parlor trick. Britt might have had a photographic memory, but Rigby knew that he had the better understanding of the spirit of the law.

KNOWING THE IMPORTANCE OF living in the moment, as the New Agers said, he dismissed all thoughts of murder and penance and concentrated on Beth's body, the way she crossed and uncrossed her legs, her lovely décolletage and the bashful way she kept trying to hide it by closing the thick white hotel robe, her left hand clutching its lapels. In an hour or so, they'd be checked out and on the way back home, and he was hoping he could work his way into her panties one more time before that. He was up a little more than four hundred dollars from the slots, and Beth was paying for the hotel since he couldn't have a Vegas hotel stay showing up on his credit card bill. Will Seghers had assured him the day before that the painting would be ready by the time he got back to Ventura, and Glenn's compliant, ethically malleable doctor had filled him in on the old fellow's steadily declining fortunes; soon, the money from the Kushik would be in his hands. He was experiencing a moment of optimism so transcendental it verged on euphoria.

Beth mopped up some of the last of her scrambled eggs

with a corner of crisp toast. "Isn't it funny how we both ordered the exact same breakfast?"

"Yeah," he said, though in fact he'd just thought what she ordered sounded good. Plus, if they both got the same thing she wouldn't try to eat off his plate, a habit that disgusted him. Paula knew well enough not to do it by this time, but on the few occasions he'd been out alone with Beth in public she'd insisted on trying whatever he'd ordered, using her fork and knife to cut his food.

"We get along pretty good, you and I."

"We do," he said. "Nice to get away like this together once in a while."

"It is. It'd be nicer if we could do it out in the open."

No. No no no no. He refused to allow himself to believe that this could be happening. "Too bad."

"If you and I were married, think of the advantages. Think of the firm, all in one piece instead of split down the middle. Think of me and the money I could put into it."

"I'm still married," he said, throat constricting.

"You could get a divorce."

"We're Catholic."

"Oh, hell, like Catholics never get divorced. Anyway I thought that was her thing, not yours."

"I made a promise right in front of God, Beth."

"You know what I think, Rigby? I think that's a really great excuse for you. Maybe I should just start dating. Plenty of guys have asked."

That sounded good to Rigby. He didn't mind sharing her at all, and if it would take off some of this newly minted pressure, terrific. In any case, marrying her would force him to reveal the extent of his financial ruin; she knew the trouble the firm was in, but not the extent to which he and Paula were underwater. He leaned across the collapsible room service table and put a hand on her bare knee. She brushed it away and readjusted the hem of the robe.

He didn't relish the thought of driving home without having released the tension in his balls. "Baby, you know I love you, and it's not going to be easy, but we can make this thing work. Let me do some thinking."

Her arms were crossed under her breasts, and he was sure she was pushing them upward for maximum effect. "Thinking's not good enough. Action."

"Action, baby. I promise, Paula and me are through. You just have to let me figure out how to do it without ruining me."

Here was another sin to confess: *Father, I lied to a woman about my intent to divorce my wife in order to entice her to commit a mortal sin with me.* It didn't seem so bad compared with the rest of his list, though, and when he saw the grudging look of faith slowly spread across her lovely fair features he knew it was worth whatever the priest could dish out.

Five minutes later she was making those grunting noises he liked so much as they writhed on the duvet, and as he ejaculated he thought, *If I died right now I'd go to hell,* which made it even better.

CHAPTER TWENTY-NINE

GLENN HASKILL SAT UP in bed, feeling better than he had in a while. The nurse's chair was empty. Most likely she was skulking about downstairs, trying to pour a drink without Nina catching her. He didn't care if she was a souse, he liked looking at her. It even occurred to him that he might have a shot at topping her when his health improved. He'd get Rigby to procure some Viagra, certain as he was that Dr. Pulliver would refuse to prescribe them on the grounds that his heart couldn't stand the strain of vigorous sexual activity. He'd heard the warnings at the end of the commercials. On the other hand, Pulliver wasn't much of a doctor, and he'd never turned any of Glenn's requests down before.

He got out of bed and, without the use of the walker, trudged to the bathroom and took a piss, dark and smelly and unsatisfactory, and moved to the sink to wash his hands. Then he looked in the mirror and had a shock.

His mustache had gone gray overnight! The tips of his wet fingers rose to touch it. He needed a shave, and he noted that the stubble above it and on his chin and cheeks had gone gray as well. And then he remembered his little secret.

He set about looking for the tin of Meltonian black, opening and emptying drawers, first in the bathroom and then in the walk-in closet, and forty-five minutes later, when the sozzled nurse crept back into the room, she found him seated in her chair by the window staring at the trees outside.

"Mr. Haskill?"

He looked up at her, jostled from a reverie about a long-dead hat-check girl at a Hollywood nightclub and how she'd liked fucking in his Bentley out behind the club after closing. She never even wanted an acting job, never asked him for a loan or anything, just liked him, and he wondered if anybody but her had ever wanted nothing from him but a good quick fuck in the back of the Bentley, and now he couldn't remember her goddamn name.

And now he couldn't remember the nurse's, either.

"What happened in here?" she asked, the scent of her boozy breath wafting to him at a distance of ten feet.

"Trying to find my Meltonian," he said, hoping that perhaps she'd failed to notice the state of his mustache.

"I'll call the girl to come straighten it up."

HE SAT IN THE study down the hall while Consuela was getting the room back into shape. Without knocking Nina came in and looked him up and down without any discernible emotion. "Looks like you're feeling better tonight."

"Never better. Wait. What do you mean tonight?"

"It's six-thirty."

"I slept all day?"

"You've been doing very little but this week."

"I don't recall sleeping more than normal."

"You have been. By the way, your nephew is coming to see you."

"My nephew? What for?"

"He's under the impression you're unwell."

It was harder than ever for him to tell when Nina was being sarcastic. She had a good deadpan, might have been a decent actress. He just nodded, and she left without further comment.

Glenn's thoughts turned to Jerry. Fond of the boy though he was, the unavoidable fact was that he was an idiot, feckless and lazy. And where Jerry was concerned, there was always the nagging guilt about his mother, Bernice, and the uncomfortable possibility—likelihood, really—that he was not merely the boy's uncle. It had been a confusing summer, spent back in St. Louis after his own Uncle Lester's death. Uncle Lester had raised the brothers after their parents' death in a Colorado train wreck, and Glenn's brother Claude was no use at all dealing with the closing of the estate.

He'd never met Bernice before Uncle Lester's funeral, having invoked the grueling 1964 pilot season (GlennCoe had no fewer than four pilots in production at the same time, three of which were picked up for the 1965 fall season) as an excuse to skip the wedding. When he finally laid eyes on her, he was shocked at her youth and beauty as much as by the notion that his blank-eyed, puffy, ashen brother had managed to snag such a prize. He'd assumed it was a question of money, but looking into the matter he found that her family—unlike his own, more recently enriched clan—was a long-standing fixture of the St. Louis Social Register, and loaded in her own right. Claude had met her at an alumni event at their old high school, he class of '38, she of '57. When they wed, he was forty-five to her twenty-six.

So it must have been love on her part. This puzzled Glenn, as he had never seen anything to admire in his older brother. But by the time Glenn returned to St. Louis, the marriage was four years old, and the bloom—for Bernice in any case—was off the rose. Claude avoided meetings with attorneys and trustees and spent his waking hours in the 2,000-square-foot basement of their Ladue mansion working on his massive HO scale train layout, an undeniably impressive operation unless you considered that a grown man of substantial means tended to it as a full-time occupation. Glenn supposed that these days he'd be diagnosed as being on some spectrum of differently abled or other, but back then he just seemed squirrely and standoffish.

He and Bernice had yielded to temptation one hot afternoon after a long and frustrating meeting at a lawyer's office. Glenn bribed a bellhop to sneak her up the service elevator of the Chase to his room, where they engaged in an athletic afternoon's worth of biblically—and, in the state of Missouri, legally—proscribed lovemaking. Listening to her talk over the next couple of weeks (these sessions continuing as they did on a daily basis) he got the impression that sexual intercourse was a rare event in their house, still more now that the initial thrill had worn off for Claude. Glenn's older brother had been, in Bernice's opinion, a virgin until his wedding night; when he'd arrived at his climax, she reported, he'd seemed stunned, even frightened.

HE SUPPOSED HE HAD let old Uncle Lester down by leaving St. Louis. He had shown them great kindness in taking him and Claude in after their parents' passing, had paid for fancy educations and gotten them started financially. But Glenn had no interest in the brick business, whereas Claude fit in just fine. Classified 4-F at the war's outset, he'd started at the company when a goodly proportion of the available pool of executives were off to fight. (Glenn had joined the Army in December of '41, as he liked to remind people, although he habitually left out the part about spending the entire war at Fort Benning.)

Poor Bernice. After she finally left Claude, she ended up with a self-styled entrepreneur who'd leveraged an Ivy League education and superficial charm and good looks into what passed for high society in St. Louis. He spent all the money she'd gotten from Claude in addition to what her own family had left. Out of sentiment, Glenn had sent her ten thousand dollars in the early nineties and instructed her never to contact him again. When Claude died he left every penny—and there were quite a few of those—to the Boy Scouts of America; only a closetful of bespoke suits, all long out of fashion, went to his son. Glenn sometimes wondered whether this had been a gesture of revenge, but in the end he believed it was because the Boy Scouts had been a wonderful adventure for the two of them in their youth, and because Claude and Jerry were roughly the same size.

As for Bernice, he supposed Jerry took care of her somehow. He never asked, but the boy was good-hearted enough to look after his own mother. Idiot or not, Glenn had always doted on young Jerry and supposed he would have even without the possibility that the lad was his own. News of a possible visit was happy indeed, and he would confirm it immediately. In addition, he resolved to be an energetic and fit host. With that in mind, he thought it would be good to get in some rest in anticipation of the arrival, and he rose from his chair, steadying himself on the desk. He was halfway across the room when his head seemed to empty itself, and he wondered why he had gotten up at all. He called out for Evvie once, then twice, louder, and at the sound of some woman shouting, "Mr. Haskill?" he fell to the carpet.

CHAPTER THIRTY

THE HOUSE WASN'T READY to sell, but it was empty and furnished, and she had the key. Keith was staring at the bedroom ceiling, his work clothes in a heap on the floor. "You ever stop and think whether what we're doing is wrong?"

"Nope. My husband does the same thing with his partner's widow and God knows who else."

"I mean with the painting."

"Oh, hell. That's nothing. Who's getting hurt?"

"That school that was supposed to get the real one."

"Keith, honey, I'm about to lose my house, which would be the end of career. I don't have the luxury of worrying about some fancy prep school losing out on a donation. When I think of all the shit I've got going on, stuff I haven't even told my priest about. Starting with you."

He looked terrified. "Why would you tell a priest about me?"

"Confession, duh. What kind of Irishman are you, anyway?"

"My mom's an atheist and my dad's a lapsed Methodist."

She sat up, leaning on her elbow. "Shut up! Your mom's not an atheist."

"She sure is."

"Will's daughter? Really?"

"Gramps is the one who drilled it into her. Gram got

super religious in her middle age. Things got real conten-
tious around that house for a few years."

"And your dad's an Irish Methodist. I've never heard of
such a thing."

"Half Irish, his mom was Methodist. My whole childhood,
we never went to church once except for my cousin's wedding."

"That sounds pretty good to me, to tell you the truth. I
probably wouldn't make the kids go or go myself if it wasn't
for Rigby."

"He's pretty serious?"

"Super serious. He goes to confession if he runs over a
squirrel. On the other hand, he doesn't see anything he
doesn't want to. When I started taking the pill ten years ago,
I didn't tell him about it and he didn't ask, I just stopped
getting pregnant and that was fine by him as long as he
didn't know the mechanics of it."

"So I guess I don't have to worry about knocking you up."

She leaned over and kissed him, his mouth tasting faintly
of the wine she poured him beforehand. "All I want from
you, baby, is orgasms and a better backswing." She sat all the
way up and assumed the lotus position.

"How much trouble do you get in for not confessing
something like that?"

"If I don't confess and get absolution I can't take Communion. So that Sunday after you first screwed me? I just
skipped Communion, but I knew Rigby'd notice if I kept
it up, so I just started going up to the altar and taking it
anyway."

"So problem solved."

She laughed, a surprised, high-pitched sound. "You really
don't know anything about this, do you? Taking Communion in a state of mortal sin is real fucking bad. If I ever do

unload all this on my priest, I'm going to be in a lot more trouble about the Communion than the adultery."

Keith frowned, puzzled at the intricacies of it all, and she found herself envying his ignorance.

WHEN SHE GOT HOME, she found Nina waiting in the driveway at the wheel of an old Mercedes of Glenn's, a black thing the size of a schooner. She didn't imagine that this would be good news, and she parked in the garage and went inside the house. Danny was off somewhere and the girls were at the pool until dinnertime, and she opened the front door and beckoned Nina inside.

"Big problem," Nina said, brushing past her in the doorway. "Haskill's chowderhead nephew's on his way here, right now."

"So?" She led her into the kitchen and took a seat at the breakfast table. "Sorry for the mess," she said, gesturing at the undone dishes from the morning and the night before.

"I didn't think he was coming. I told him his uncle was sick, like, three or four days ago. He hemmed and hawed about how expensive it was to fly out here on short notice, and I didn't offer to have Haskill pay for it. I thought he was going to stay put, but now I get a call he's on his way in from Ontario. I've been trying to get Rigby all afternoon but he isn't picking up."

"No, he wouldn't, he went to Vegas with his whore."

Nina looked shocked, which pleased Paula. "He told you that?"

"He didn't have to."

Nina cocked her head in puzzled admiration. "Well. When he gets back, or starts answering his phone, we need to figure out what we're doing. I don't want the nephew and Haskill giving each other ideas about the painting."

"We don't need Rigby. You have the nephew's number?"

CHAPTER THIRTY-ONE

"FUCK, FUCK, FUCK!" HE screamed at the bright GPS display on the dash of the rented Lexus, the fifth such outburst in the last half hour. He could actually feel his blood pressure rising, a tingling, electrical sensation in his fingertips as he drummed them on the steering wheel— piano black, with an optional heating element that might have made sense back in St. Louis—and he thought about the beta blockers his doctor had prescribed specifically for the LA traffic. They were ensconced safely in his carry-on, locked in the trunk, and perfectly inaccessible unless he dared take an exit ramp onto some unknown, doubtless gang-ridden street.

He had been assured that not only was flying into Ontario cheaper than LAX or Burbank, it was practically speaking not much farther than either alternative. But today, the traffic had started slowing almost the minute he left the airport. By the time he hit Pomona, it had slowed to twenty-five, by West Covina fifteen, when it was moving at all. The accursed GPS showed the 10 Freeway into downtown LA a solid mass of red and estimated a seven-hour drive to Santa Barbara, and he scanned the AM radio for some explanation until he happened upon a honeyed baritone describing in loving detail a cataclysmic wreck downtown involving seven passenger vehicles and a tractor-trailer, three of the former ablaze. The reporter was hovering above the pandemonium in a helicopter and sounded energized if not positively thrilled at the standstill of the various freeway lanes, casting aspersions at the passing rubberneckers, whom he described as "looky-loos," an unfamiliar phrase that filled Jerry with still more unreasonable anger.

When his phone trilled, he picked it up without bothering to check the caller's identity. "What?" he said. "What do you want?"

"Jerry?" said an unfamiliar voice, sounding a bit shocked.

"Sorry. Not your fault. Having a hard afternoon. Who's this?"

"Paula Rigby. I heard you were coming into town."

Paula Rigby. His blood pressure rose a bit higher, and he could feel his face flushing. Inexplicably married to his uncle's sleazeball lawyer, she was one of the most fascinating women he'd ever met. Classy, smart, well-read, well-dressed, she was also tall and willowy with a lovely long throat, and she smelled nice, something sharp and floral that seemed to come from her pores rather than from any sort of chemical potion. That she was married to a sleazy creep like Rigby was unbearable. That was the way it always happened, wasn't it? The loveliest creatures ended up with thuggish jerks who treated them like shit, while nice guys like him went unappreciated.

"Jerry?" she said. "Are you there?"

"Right. Sorry, I'm driving."

"I don't want to cause a wreck or anything."

"No, I'm fine, it's this damn stop-and-go. I'm not going to get into Santa Barbara until midnight at least."

"That's what I'm calling about, I want you to stay with us."

"That's fine, I'm going to stay with my uncle."

"Jerry, he's not up to having any company. And we're only half an hour away, I promise it'll be better than that musty old house, the whole place smells like a sickroom these days anyway."

"I don't want to put you out. I can stay in a hotel."

"Don't be ridonculous. It'll be fun, I promise."

Ridonculous. She was even funny! He knew it was hopeless, he was going to do anything she told him to. "Okay."

"I'll text you the address."

THE TRAFFIC IN DOWNTOWN LA had thinned considerably by the time he hit the 170, and it was only eight forty-five when he pulled into the Rigbys' driveway up in the hills above Ventura. Paula opened the front door and waved, and he got halfway out and called to her. "All right if I park here for now?"

"It's fine, Rigby's stuck in LA overnight. Need help with your bags?"

"I'm good," he said. He felt like a seventh-grader with a crush on a sophomore. Stupid to get so excited at the news that Rigby wouldn't be there. What did he think, that she was going to creep into his room in the middle of the night and confess that she'd always found him irresistible? He happened to know that the Rigbys were practicing Catholics, and a small wave of shame washed over his soul.

Stupid, stupid, stupid. He slung his bag over his shoulder and approached the front door, where Paula wrapped him in a warmer hug than he might reasonably have hoped for. He tried for an expression of friendly but indifferent insouciance as he returned it.

Once she'd shown him to the guest room, she led him into the kitchen, where she poured him a glass of red wine—Shiraz, she said—and served him a plate of assorted cheeses and fancy crispy wafers to spread them on.

"These are delicious," he said, wishing he could think of something witty or articulate to say instead.

"Oh, it's nothing. I thought maybe I'd take you to dinner, since it's just the two of us. The kids eat early."

"You don't have to do that."

"I know I don't. But I don't really have any grown-up food to fix, and you must be starving. It's, what, ten-something your time?"

He was, in fact, starving, and he could picture himself eating the entire plate of cheese and making a fool of himself. Maybe in a restaurant, he could muster some of the suave persona he knew dwelt inside him.

THE RESTAURANT WAS WEST of the Rigbys' neighborhood, down in the flat part of town not far from the ocean, in a former house, and the sun was low in the sky when they took their table on the deck behind the house. "This is the best food in Ventura, has been for a long time," Paula said. "So, you got stuck in the same jam Rigby did?"

"Is that what happened to him?"

"He was coming in from Vegas." She rolled her eyes in disdain on the last word.

"Traffic was getting better by the time I got there."

"Well. Maybe he just felt like spending the night in LA. Who knows."

"It was pretty hairy starting from when I left Ontario."

"You flew into Ontario?"

"You make it sound terrible."

"No, it's just so far away, and the 10 is a miserable drive."

"Wouldn't have been so bad if passing through downtown hadn't been such a mess."

"How come you didn't just take the 605 to the 210? You would have backtracked a little, but you still would have saved time."

He knew she wasn't attacking him, and he admired her

resourcefulness and know-how, but he felt defensive none-theless and had to force himself to stifle the instinct.

"Just went where the GPS told me to go," he said.

"I'm sorry, we get so obsessed with traffic around here everybody thinks they've got a better way for you to get any-where."

"So, what looks good?" he said, reaching across the table and tapping her menu.

The waitress appeared at his shoulder before she had a chance to answer and asked the same question in the same words, which caused him to snap his head in her direction in shock. Did this young woman have the temerity to mock a customer to his face?

But Paula laughed. "Don't give him any grief, Sherry, he just had a rough day on the freeway."

"I'm sorry," the young woman said, putting a friendly hand on his shoulder.

"It's okay," he said, anxious to seem like the good sport he had never really been able to force himself to be.

Paula asked about the preparation of the fish special, and as the two of them batted the subject back and forth he considered Paula's special gracefulness. Even next to this attractive young woman, she stood out as some-thing very special, and he was regarding her pale throat with longing when he noticed the women snickering, not unkindly.

"Hello, Jerry?"

"Sorry," he said. "I'll have the KC strip, medium well."

"Gotcha," the waitress said, and started to turn.

"Wait," Paula said. "Medium *well?*"

On her face was a friendly, teasing smile, but his face began to get warm. His ex-wife had been this way, never let him order a steak the way he wanted it. He liked it gray, but he couldn't bear to have Paula think the less of him right now. "On second thought, medium."

The waitress smiled and jotted down the change, and when she left Paula apologized. "I'm sorry. But Rigby does the same thing, and I can't stand to watch him eat it."

"Yeah, you're right. Just force of habit."

BACK AT THE RIGBYS', she asked if he wanted to go to sleep or watch a movie with her. He was exhausted from the trip and sleepy from the food and wine, but he said yes.

"I had one picked out, but it's kind of a chick flick. If you want to pick something else, that's fine."

"Whatever you want to watch is fine with me," he said as she handed him his fifth glass of wine of the evening and steered him toward the big couch in what she referred to as the media room, one that faced a gigantic television screen. "I'll probably fall asleep halfway through anyway."

CHAPTER THIRTY-TWO

"IN CASE YOU HADN'T noticed, I'm fucking furious." She wasn't being coy about it, lips pursed so tight she looked like she was trying to keep a canary from escaping her mouth, eyes squinting as though staring straight into a dust storm.

"I did notice."

"I don't understand checking into a four-star hotel and then checking out before we even get to go to bed."

"Baby, I told you, it's a client thing, I have to get back to Ventura. I'm doing it for the firm. For us." He stretched his hand across to her knee, but she brushed it away.

"Don't you fucking touch me. That was a three-hundred-fifty-dollar room. Which, I'll remind you, I paid for myself."

Jesus God, could her temperament ever turn shitty at the slightest provocation. When they'd hit the slowdown into LA that afternoon, she'd instantly switched on the bitching, addressing it straight at him, as though Rigby himself had arranged for a big rig to plow right into a bunch of passenger vehicles on purpose with the express purpose of fucking up her ride back to Ventura. It was about four o'clock when he suggested—despite the fact that traffic was starting to get moving again—that they just say fuck it and check into a nice hotel in Santa Monica, and as soon as he'd said it she sweetened right up.

Rigby tried to imagine what marriage to Beth would be

like. Constant demands, incessant suspicions, no end to the carping. He didn't want to leave that fucking hotel room either. But all morning his assistant had been trying to get him on his cell, and frankly, he hadn't wanted to talk to Lena about anything, important or not. The only important news he could imagine was Glenn Haskill's death, and if that was it, the old bastard would still be dead tomorrow. And since the phone was close to dead, he let the battery run down to nothing. And then he checked into the hotel and recharged the fucking thing and found out that Haskill's grasping imbecile nephew was not only coming into town practically unannounced, but staying at his own house. Shit. He should have told Lena to text him if it was anything important. Now he had no option but to decamp and head straight for home.

That was what Beth couldn't understand, the urgency of his return. He couldn't tell her anything about wanting to keep Jerry away from the painting, of course, but there was a more important consideration, and one that he absolutely couldn't let Beth know was something that concerned him in the slightest. Jerry Haskill wanted to fuck Paula, and though he didn't think she would take him up on it, he knew he was on shaky ground of late, and it was always possible she might decide to take vengeance on him by sleeping with the schmuck, who, after all, was going to be a reasonably rich man before long.

He cursed himself for the last thought. It couldn't be said that Paula didn't care about money, but he knew she wouldn't fuck for it, either. He'd have to confess that uncharitable thought, he told himself, and then he considered that he had several things he wasn't quite ready to confess yet.

Cresting over the hill just past Thousand Oaks, he realized Beth was still talking to him. He'd shut her out completely without even realizing he was doing it. With Paula that never happened, even when she was going at him at full-gale force, cutting him to pieces. He wondered why that was, and it came to him that when Paula yelled, she was still saying something worth listening to, as opposed to just giving him shit for the sake of giving him shit. *A woman worthy of respect and love,* he thought, and for a split second he felt something akin to guilt for the Vegas jaunt, for the whole sordid business with Beth. Then his attention was diverted by the sound of Beth's voice, a steady, sharp, piercing thing when she was animated and angry, not unlike a parrot's. She didn't sound like that most of the time, or did she? He wasn't around her most of the time. And evidently they'd arrived at the point where she felt free to speak to him this way, with no fear of rejection. Jesus, what had he been thinking back in Vegas, telling her he'd marry her? Even if it were possible, it was plain to him now that such a marriage would be the ninth circle of hell. Was that the lake of fire or the fecal pool? Either way. Didn't matter. He had to find a way to cool this thing down. She was just getting down to her own most important piece of leverage against him now, and he found himself feeling the first stirrings of panic.

"And I will shut that firm down if I need to, Rigby. To be honest, my CPA is giving me a lot of shit about it anyway. A law firm with one client? Come on."

"It's not my fault you married a guy who thought he was an extra-special adventure athlete or whatever the fuck he called it."

"Extreme sportsman. And how dare you bring up Britt's death at a time like this?"

"Hey, if he hadn't taken a stupid risk, the firm would be in fine shape."

"And I suppose you'd prefer that."

"Have my best friend and law partner alive? Of course I would," he said, even as he sensed it wasn't exactly the right answer.

"You're telling me you're not even a little glad we can be together?"

Paula was always telling him he was a glib son of a bitch, and he took no small amount of pride in his ability to bullshit on the fly, but by God here he lacked a satisfactory response, and he just took a deep breath, let it settle in his lungs, then slowly blew it out to give himself a few seconds to think of something.

Nothing. There was no response that wasn't going to get him in deeper.

"You spineless creep. All I am to you is a piece of ass."

Now there was a straight line worthy of Bud Abbott, real low-hanging fruit, and instead of voicing any of the various callous ripostes that sprang immediately to his tongue, he let out a big, loud laugh, at which she took an umbrella off of the floor and brought it down on his head, a left-handed blow that landed with surprising force. He lost momentary control of the vehicle and drifted into the left-hand lane, provoking angry honking from a tiny, ancient, once-white Datsun. When he managed to swerve back into position, he waved apologetically and insincerely at the white-haired lady behind the wheel, who flipped him off anyway, then turned to Beth.

"You really are one crazy bitch, you know that? You just about killed us both."

"The amount of disrespect—"

"You know what? Shut the fuck up."

"How fucking dare you?"

"You heard me. I don't want to hear another goddamned word until we get back to Ventura."

APPARENTLY, THE BARELY CONTAINED rage he felt had manifested itself in his voice, because to his great surprise, for the rest of the drive she stared out the window and said nothing. That got him worried about a possible explosion back at her house, but when he dropped her off there and picked up his own SUV, which they'd hidden in her garage, she kept quiet. She walked into the house without a word, without any hints about whether she was hurt or just pissed off or some particular combination of both, and that in itself was a relief. He'd been afraid she wouldn't let him return home to Paula without oaths of fealty being sworn, among other insincere promises that certainly would have qualified as exaggerations if not outright lies.

He walked into the house quietly, disarmed the alarm system and crept toward the media room, where he heard the TV playing. There, he found Jerry Haskill sound asleep, snoring quietly on the couch while next to him Paula watched the movie that had knocked him out.

"How was your trip?" Paula asked without looking up or pausing.

"Fine," he said. On-screen, a pair of young and improbably pretty actors in 1940s clothing wept in one another's arms, the girl pleading as the boy prepared to enter an Army recruiting station. "What are you watching this for? You hate this kind of shit."

"Shhh," she said, a finger to her freshly glossed lips, indicating Jerry.

He took a good look at his wife. She was wearing a lightweight, clingy lavender dress and heels; not unusual attire for working hours or a party, but unheard of in the evening at home. He found the jealousy rising in his throat and was about to say something stupid and accusatory when she spoke again.

"You two have a good time?"

For the second time that night, he was at a loss for a response.

"You going straight to bed, or you want to watch the rest of this with Jerry and me?" She was looking at the screen as she said it.

There was no malice in her voice. Maybe that was the result of having the upper hand for once, he thought. Or maybe he'd heard wrong? "Bed," he said. "Long drive."

She glanced at him briefly, not deigning to offer even the slightest of insincerely polite smiles. "Night."

IN THE MORNING, HE made an excuse to Jerry about his uncle's condition and headed up the 101 to determine whether or not Glenn was going to be lucid when they finally connected. Nina took him upstairs and gestured toward the bed, where the old man took in shallow breaths and looked through red, rheumy, half-closed eyes at him with no sign of recognition. A pale redheaded nurse sat in the corner of the room reading a thick paperback, looking half pickled herself and breathing loudly through her mouth.

"Look, Mr. Haskill, it's Mr. Rigby," Nina said, loud and slow.

Haskill didn't respond. His skin looked papery, veins blue beneath the scalp, and Rigby almost felt bad for having wished he'd get on with it and die so he could get busy selling the painting. He did harbor a certain fondness for his client, after all, and a degree of gratitude for the fact that he alone hadn't bailed on what was left of the firm.

He followed Nina down the stairs, and when they reached the kitchen he asked her about the nurse. "Is she hammered?"

"Her? Twenty-four hours a day. You want her fired?"

"No, let's keep her on. Don't want any bad feelings around here, do we?"

"I guess not. You want the nephew to see him?"

"No reason he shouldn't, I guess. Glenn's not going to understand anything, is he?"

"Not a chance. Make sure he comes before four o'clock, the GP's sending over a nephrologist."

"A what?"

"A kidney specialist."

"No fucking way. A specialist who makes house calls?"

"Dr. Pulliver pulls some weight in the medical community up here. And this kidney guy was a big fan of *High Cimarron* when he was a kid. So he's coming in person, see if he can't do something to make him more comfortable and avoid an ambulance trip."

Rigby nodded, wished once again that the old bastard would hurry up and croak, then a moment later felt bad again and made a note to add that to his ever-lengthening confession.

LENA GAVE HIM THE stink eye when he walked into the office at three, and as was his habit he pretended not to notice. "If you don't start picking up your phone when I call, I'm going to quit."

"Sorry, phone died while I was driving back, and I didn't have my car charger."

"I'm not talking about yesterday, I'm talking about today."

"Right. I was at the old man's house in conference." He passed by her as she stood. She really looked pissed off this time.

"Wait."

He pushed his door open and found Stony sitting right there at his desk, arms folded across his big chest.

"I was trying to tell you," Lena said.

"And what's wrong with the waiting area?" he asked her.

"That's my reception area, and I didn't like the way he

was looking at me." She gave Stony a transitory sidelong glance before looking away, flustered.

"All right, get back to your desk." She returned to her post and he shut the door. He was about to tell Stony to get the fuck out of his chair, but seeing the expression on the man's face, or lack thereof, he thought better of it. No need to escalate yet. He turned on the white noise machine sitting on the floor lest Lena catch wind of whatever damning accusations were about to fly.

"I told you not to mess with this kind of business," Stony said.

"What are you talking about, Stony?"

"I'm not fucking around here. I need to know what you did with that gun afterwards."

Jesus, but Stony was a big man. A fair amount of flab around the muscle but Rigby knew from his days in competition that the core underneath was solid, and he imagined that Stony had been in more than his share of fights. "The gun you sold me?"

"I told you once I'm not fucking around. Magda Schuller was a friend of my wife's, she worked at the clinic."

"Doesn't mean anything to me. You saying you want the gun back?"

"Are you trying to be funny?"

"Not at all."

"Radio says they found a gun on the so-called killer's person. That wouldn't be the same one, would it?"

"I don't know what you're talking about, Stony."

Stony got up out of Rigby's chair. "This better not get back to me. Meaning you best not get caught." He walked out of the office, scowling at Lena as he passed her desk, and she blanched visibly, which almost made the whole exchange worth it for Rigby.

CHAPTER THIRTY-THREE

THE MORNING NURSE WAS a chunky man with long, thick, blond sideburns. Like the drunken redhead, he sat in the corner chair reading, ignoring Nina and Haskill and waiting for the vital signs monitor to indicate some abnormality or an alarm to signal time for medication. Nina was seated in a heavy armchair with embroidered upholstery next to the bed; Haskill had bought it at auction for more than twenty grand—he couldn't remember how much more—because it had once been John Wayne's. Bidding had started at eight hundred dollars, and Haskill had gotten himself into a stubborn pissing match with Maury Staines, a former protégé–turned-rival. Staines still had programs on TV, which Haskill watched obsessively, offering a running commentary on their subpar production values, rehashed scripts, dull actors and all-around shoddiness. To Nina, they seemed exactly like everything else on TV, but Haskill's accompanying rants made them bearable, almost entertaining.

Her feelings this morning were a complex mix of relief and frustration. The former stemmed from the old man's sudden recovery, the result of the nephrologist's intervention. This reversal had made her doubt the GP's competence; when she mentioned this to Rigby, he'd nodded and, after a thoughtful pause, said, "This could work to our advantage."

This notion, she thought, should have filled her with revulsion and shame, but she'd had to admit that it was true.

"Goddamned if I don't feel like a new man," Haskill said, sitting up in his bed. He'd applied the black Meltonian to the pencil mustache once again; seeing it fade back to a wispy dishwater-gray had been one of the first and most alarming signs of his deterioration. "Did I dream it, or did my nephew come to see me yesterday?"

"He was here, he's staying down in Ventura with the Rigbys."

"The whole last week feels like a hallucination. Why isn't he staying here?"

"You were doing so badly we didn't think you should have visitors."

"Doing better now, he'll stay here tonight."

"We'll see what the doctor says." The plan was to keep Jerry at as much distance from Haskill as possible.

A COUPLE OF HOURS later, Haskill surprised Nina by going downstairs for lunch. "Where's Jerry? Thought you called and asked him for lunch."

"He had plans to visit Solvang with Mrs. Rigby. You'll see him for dinner."

The old man leveled an evil smirk at her. "I can understand. That Paula's something else entirely. He thinks he's going to make her, doesn't he? He's in for a surprise. That Paula's got eyes for nobody but Rigby."

"Won't hurt the boy to dream," Nina said.

THAT EVENING, SHE STEPPED into the busy gloom of the Town Crier and squinted. Rigby was nowhere among the crowd at the bar, so she ordered a whiskey sour from a woman who seemed to take an instant dislike to her.

"Five dollars," the woman said, setting the drink down. Nina gave her a five and no tip, then retreated to a booth against the opposite wall. She was absently checking her email when a figure appeared at her left.

"You work for Rigby, right?"

She started, and looking up saw a young man whose face was familiar in the vaguest way. "No."

"I met you at my gramps's house. I'm Keith."

"Oh."

"Mind if I sit down?"

"I'm meeting someone."

"Just until they get here?" He sat without waiting for a reply.

She noted the bartender's disapproving stare and assumed she had designs on this Keith, who struck Nina as a genial dolt. "I suppose you might as well."

"So you don't work for Rigby. You've got something to do with this painting business though, right?"

"Not so loud," she said, her initial impression confirmed.

"Sorry."

"I work for Mr. Haskill, the owner of the painting."

"Right. That's what I meant."

"And what do you do again?"

"Golf pro."

"Ah. Must be nice. Outdoors all the time."

He looked at the ceiling and pursed his lips, considering his response with care. "Yeah, but I'm assistant manager of the pro shop, so there's a lot of inside time, too. In the long run, I'd like to get into course management, which is where there's room for advancement."

It had been a long time since she'd been in a bar by herself, and the absurd notion struck that he was hitting on her. Surely not.

"So you work for the old TV producer guy. Are you married?"

By God, he was. She looked him up and down and, finding him moderately appealing physically, wondered what it would take for her to get over the dolt factor. "No, not anymore."

"I was wondering if you'd like to maybe go out sometime."

She hit the telephone icon. "What's your number, Keith?"

He rattled it off and she punched it into the phone. "I'll call you when I've got some free time." The bartender was staring daggers at her, and when Nina smiled back at her, she turned away.

Keith was looking pleased with himself and drained half his Budweiser in a triumphant swig. He turned toward the front door when Nina signaled to Rigby, who had just entered, and looked like he was going to spit it out again.

Rigby stopped at the bar and flirted with the bartender, who seemed even more taken with him than with Keith. He jerked his head toward the booth, and her expression soured for a brief moment before resuming its original adoring state.

"I guess I'll leave you to it," Keith said, rising.

But Rigby was upon them, holding two bottles of beer and another whiskey sour. "Hey, you can't leave, I just got here." He put a hand on Keith's back, and the younger man looked terrified.

"We do have a business meeting," Nina said.

"Yeah, but this is good timing. I need your help, Keith, buddy."

Keith knocked back the dregs of his beer and accepted the new one from Rigby. "Thanks."

She studied their interaction with a clinician's detachment. Keith was profoundly ill at ease in Rigby's presence, and Rigby seemed not to pick up on it at all.

"All right. In a couple of days I'm flying up to San Fran to talk to an auction house man I'm told has a strong connection with the Russian market, who might be willing to break some rules as long as the money's right."

"Okay," Nina said.

"Now I've got a variation on the plan. Needs your grandpa's cooperation, but it's fucking brilliant. Ready? Three paintings."

Keith nodded in perfect, blank incomprehension. Nina squeezed her eyes shut. "No. This is too complicated already."

"Hear me out. Jerry Haskill wants to see the painting. I told him I put it into a safe-deposit box in LA."

Nina shook her head. "Why LA?"

"Because it makes it more complicated for him to get to see it. I told him only the main Bank of America branch in Beverly Hills has the right climate-controlled vault. He's a dumb shit so he bought it. I've actually got both paintings at the office. It'll buy us a day or two, I'm feeding him a big guilt trip about not spending time with sick old Uncle Glenn."

"Buy us a day or two for what?" Nina said.

"Look. Both of our pictures are passable, right?"

"A real Kushik and a great forgery," Keith said, and Rigby winced.

"Not so loud," Rigby said. "So your grandpa can paint us another, less passable one, and that's the one that goes to the school. If they never tumble to it, great. If they figure out it's bogus, it just means old Evvie got sold a bill of goods back in the day."

Nina finished her first whiskey sour and nodded. "And we sell the real one and the portrait of Mrs. Kushik to some Russian billionaire."

"Meanwhile tomorrow I go to LA and rent an actual safe-deposit box, and we put one of the fakes in it so we can show it to the idiot. Hopefully the sloppy one, so I can tell this auctioneer I've got my hands on two Kushiks." Rigby put his hand on Keith's shoulder. "Think the old man will go for it?"

Shrinking from Rigby's touch, Keith nodded. "I'll see if I can't talk him into it." Then he made an excuse, left his half-full bottle of beer on the table and walked out the front door.

"He's a funny guy, isn't he?" Rigby said.

"He asked me on a date."

"Yeah? Good for you." He gave her a funny, appraising look and didn't say anything, just took a long pull of his beer, and Nina noticed that the bartender was giving her the stink eye again.

CHAPTER THIRTY-FOUR

THE REFRIGERATOR MOTOR STARTED humming while his grandfather sat at the kitchen table considering the request in silence. Finally he let out a bitter chuckle and spoke. "Jesus, that greedy son of a bitch." He shook his head at the effrontery of it. "Here I did the damn near impossible, made him a Kushik indistinguishable from a real one, and he wants more. How come he doesn't ask me himself?"

"I think it's an idea he just had. I ran into him at the Town Crier. He was meeting that woman who works for the old guy. Nina."

Another contemptuous shake of the head. "Again, that greedy son of a bitch."

"How do you mean?"

"I mean to hear you tell it, that wife of his is some kind of knockout, and here he is on the side topping some girl he barely knows."

"I don't think that's what it was."

"Then why's he meeting her at a bar?"

"I don't know. Anyway, I asked her out myself."

"You did?"

"You sound surprised."

He twisted his features, purplish lower lip extended in puzzlement. "Just didn't strike me as your type. Kind of stern. Buttoned-down."

"Yeah, I don't know what it was, she just seemed interesting, sitting there by herself. She didn't exactly say yes or no."

He looked off into the distance and took a deep breath. "All right. You sit tight here for a minute and I'll show you something." The old man rose, wincing at a pain in his knee, picked up a wooden chair and took it into the hallway. Standing on it he released the trapdoor leading to the attic and pulled down the folding ladder with a shriek of corroded steel. "Hold on a minute," he yelled into the parlor, and Keith sat looking at his phone, wondering whether he should have asked Nina out. For all he knew his grandfather was right, she was screwing Rigby, who now had one more reason to beat the shit out of him if he found out.

There was loud clomping as his grandfather went up the ladder, then a thumping on the ceiling and the sound of furniture being moved, then a bang and a muffled "God-fucking-damnit."

He stood and went into the hallway. "Gramps?"

"I'm fine," his grandfather said, enraged and unseen. "Go sit down like I told you."

He returned to the parlor and sat. He was about twelve when he'd watched his grandmother hectoring his grandfather over his language, in particular his taking the various names of the Lord in vain. Gramps's reaction had been stoic, up to a point, and then he'd turned to young Keith and said, "Jesus Christ on a pogo stick, did you ever hear such a crock of shit in your life?" This had moved his grandmother to storm out of the house without a further word, and Keith understood now that his grandfather had been drinking that day. The whole incident had horrified and thrilled him, and he wondered how the two of them had managed to share a house together all those decades, loathing one another as they had.

Now came more bumping and thumping as the old man came down the ladder, more sounds of tortured metal as he replaced it, and a loud grunt as he slammed the trapdoor shut. He reappeared in the kitchen holding a large oil on canvas, a wooded river scene, and he laid it down on the table.

"This might do it. I'm not painting any more of these, but this is one I did when I first started studying with Kushik. It's a pretty good imitation and I didn't sign it."

"Where's that?"

"Ventura River, up in Ojai. River was running high and I wanted to paint some moving water the way he did. Not a great picture, but it might fool a casual glance, and in the end Rigby doesn't care if the school eventually figures out it's a fraud."

"I think he was pretty set on you painting a new one."

"He's going to have to learn to settle."

IT WAS ONLY NINE and he didn't want to go home yet. He thought about calling Mo and seeing if he could come over, then decided to just show up, figuring he stood a better chance of success in person. She lived above a little furniture store on Thompson east of downtown, and he parked on the street and climbed the back stairs to the apartment door. When she came to the door she didn't smile, but she waved him in, apparently still mad about the missed weekend at Big Bear. Her affect was sufficiently cold to keep him from attempting a kiss as a greeting. "Want a beer?" she asked.

He opened the refrigerator and looked over the selection. Nothing he or she usually drank, just expensive craft beers with ironic, retro labels. He took out an IPA, opened it and went into her tiny living room, where she sat in the easy chair facing the couch. The warm light from her floor lamp brought out the color of her hair and gave her complexion a ruddier than usual look. He understood that he was in some kind of trouble, and she looked so lovely at that moment that he wondered about taking her seriously, breaking it off for good with Paula, making plans for the future. He was thirty-four years old, and it was time he stopped treading water. He sat on the couch and waited in vain for her to say something until her pitiless stare got to him and he spoke.

"So, Big Bear. Fun?"

"Oh, yeah."

"Swim?"

"Yep."

"Hike?"

"Yep."

That was all he was going to get. "So you're still mad."

"Nope. If I was mad I wouldn't have let you in. Anyway, why would I be mad?"

"Because I didn't go to Big Bear?"

"Or maybe because you haven't called since I got back? Or stepped into the grill to say hi?"

Jesus. How long had she been back, anyway? "Sorry."

"Or maybe because Chloe saw you going into a vacant house with one of your students?"

He fancied that he could actually feel the blood draining from his face. "She what?"

"A member she recognized. A realtor. She lives with her parents down the street, saw you and asked me if maybe you were buying a house. I said are you nuts? Keith? Buy a house? She said yeah, he must be taking it seriously, they were in there for an hour at least."

For a split second he considered saying that yes, in fact, he was thinking about buying a house, but the amount of lying he'd already done was making him feel queasy. "I'm not proud of myself."

"Wow, that's really impressive, Keith. Not proud. Well, guess what? She told me this while we were in Big Bear. Know what? I wasn't surprised. Even though it hadn't occurred to me that you might be messing around, it didn't surprise me, because I've known for a while that you didn't really give a shit about me. And you know what else? There was a guy there, a friend of Amy's husband's. He's in dental school. A guy with ambitions. And guess what else? He's my own age. That beer you're drinking is one of his."

He nodded, trying desperately to act as though this was all okay by him. "That's great. I'm happy for you."

"Well, that's sweet. Anyway, I'm sure you're disappointed about the booty call not working out the way you planned, but now you're fully informed, so I'm asking you to finish the beer and go."

"Right." He stood and tried to think of something apologetic that wouldn't actually make things worse; failing this, he gave a half-assed wave and went to the back door again.

"Hey, Keith?" she called out as he opened the door. "I'm going to do you a favor you don't deserve."

"What's that?"

"Not turning you into HR for fucking a member."

He gave her an appreciative nod and headed outside and down the stairs into the alley, where a pair of noisy cats were mating in the bushes. One of them howled and bolted, shaking leaves and flying past his feet with a plaintive, anguished howl. The golden eyes of the other glowed resentment at him from within the shrub. "Sorry, kitty-cats."

CHAPTER THIRTY-FIVE

WITHOUT HER EYES EVER leaving the road she knew his were on her legs. They were just passing Camarillo, a good forty-five minutes before they got to the bank given the traffic, and Jerry Haskill would not shut the fuck up. She usually found that a bore would quiet down once they realized that the target of their monologue wasn't paying attention, but Jerry seemed to have no inkling that she wasn't enthralled by his observations on modern American life and marriage.

"People just don't listen to one another the way they used to. My ex, Valerie, you met her a while back when things were still good, she used to sit there not listening to a word I was saying. I'd say something that caught her ear and she'd say, 'Sorry, what were you saying?' Drove me crazy. And then she had an affair with our insurance guy, which is what happens when couples stop communicating in a healthy way. You know how I found out she was having an affair?"

It took her a moment to understand that he expected an answer. "Text messages?"

"Did I tell you this story already?"

"That's how people always find out. If you're having an affair, you shouldn't ever text about it."

"I was home early from a trip to Kansas City. I thought I'd surprise her. She was taking a shower and her phone buzzed.

I looked down at it, just a reflex, you know, like you do when you hear the buzz. And it said, 'I can't wait to taste your pussy tonight.' Our insurance man! And I scrolled up and found all these other filthy messages. One of them said—" He stopped, his throat closing up, and waited a few seconds before continuing. "One of them said how she couldn't wait to get him into our bed again. Our own bed, Paula."

"That's awful," she said. *More like awful stupid*, she thought. What was wrong with that woman?

"She came out of the bathroom in her robe and saw me holding the phone and slapped me. She slapped me and said, 'How dare you read my texts!' and I just stood there."

"That's a really sad story, Jerry."

"Well, I'd never have an affair."

"Good for you."

"I mean if I was married, I wouldn't." His voice deepened. "As a single man I have plenty of relationships. Sometimes with married women, but if I were married again I would never cheat on my wife."

"That's admirable."

"I'm sure you would never either."

Jesus. For a laugh she thought about reaching over and putting her hand on his knee, but no, that would have been cruel. "I'm glad you hold such a high opinion of me."

"Do you think Rigby would ever have one?"

"If he did I wouldn't know. He's very clever and I'm very trusting."

That finally shut him up for a few minutes. She sped up and moved into the passing lane to get ahead of a Porsche doing 63 and worked hard to suppress a smile at his struggle not to come right out and tell her about Rigby's well-known infidelities. After the story about the texts she felt a whiff of pity for him, and a smaller one of guilt; even if his deepest motive was to break up her marriage, at least he was siding with her against her cheating husband.

Finally, passing Calabasas, he spoke again. "I got the last laugh, though. The guy divorced his wife and he and Val got married and three years later he dumped her for another one of his clients. I hear she was devastated."

"There you go, Jerry, there's always a bright spot somewhere."

THE BANK WAS AN imposing structure in downtown Beverly Hills, a massive façade that announced to the world that this was no mere branch location but a place of importance where the wealthy and celebrated could entrust their money and valuables. So it seemed anyway to Paula, who felt inadequate as she and Jerry walked into the vaulted lobby and approached an oaken desk the size of a sedan.

"We'd like to see the contents of this deposit box, please," she said to a constipated-looking young man, offering him her identification and the paperwork for the box.

He scanned the documents, nostrils flared, then looked up and smiled. "Absolutely, Mrs. Rigby. I'm Alan Blick, I was the one who helped your husband in securing Mr. Haskill's space." Her sense of alienation dissipated as he rose and beckoned them with a finger crooked over his shoulder. "I very much enjoyed meeting him. And would this be Mr. Haskill?"

"I'm his nephew," Jerry said. He looked like a little boy, and sounded as cowed as she'd felt when they walked in. *Fear of authority,* she thought. *Good to know.*

"Mr. Rigby certainly made an impression here. He's certainly dedicated to Mr. Haskill's interests and security."

He led them to an empty room and bade them sit at a long table before disappearing, locking the door behind him. Paula was seated as close to Jerry as she could get without actually touching him, and she could feel the tension radiating from his back, as though he were in the waiting room about to have a tooth pulled. "Are you okay?" she asked.

"I'm fine." His eyes were fixed on the blank wall, painted a soothing yellow.

She let it drop.

Then he half-whispered, as though they were in a library or a church. "You know what else Val did with him that I found out about in those damned texts?"

"What?" she whispered back in the same low, velvet tone.

"Anal intercourse. That was always an issue between us, she absolutely refused. And then I find out that she's been letting him in there for months."

What had changed between them that had led him to feel so free to talk dirty with her? She couldn't imagine him, on any of his earlier trips to SoCal, bringing up this sort of thing. In fact, she'd considered him a bit of a prude, reddening when Rigby swore in front of women and using euphemisms like "bullcrap," and now here he was talking about his ex-wife getting cornholed in his own bed. She wasn't sure whether she liked this Jerry better than the old one or not.

She was about to say something noncommittal when Alan Blick returned with a guard, the latter wheeling a large cart that carried a large metal box. From the lower level of the cart he took a small easel, which he set up at the end of the table. "All right, time to take a look. Firstly, do you mind if Delmore and I remain in the room?"

"Not at all," she said, and nodded at the guard, who put on a pair of cotton gloves before unlocking and opening the box. Then he reached inside from above and extracted the painting, shrouded in velvet, which he removed as Alan manipulated a control panel on the wall. A warm light fell on the easel and the guard carefully placed the painting thereupon.

"It's beautiful," she said, surprising herself. She couldn't put her finger on the precise reason, but she liked it more than the other two.

"So that cruddy little picture's worth a fortune, huh?" Jerry said.

THEY TOOK THE PCH back to Ventura afterward and stopped at a seaside restaurant south of Malibu for lunch. Their table was on the deck overlooking the beach, densely populated for a Wednesday, and Jerry was quiet as they waited for their food to arrive, staring pensively at the ocean behind his mirrored shades. A warm breeze blew in off the water, and he let out a sigh. She thought he was going to say something, but his attention was captured by a limping dog chasing a frisbee thrown by a man with a heartbroken look wearing a filthy, bedraggled LA Rams sweatsuit. When at length the waitress returned with their salads, Jerry looked almost as miserable. When she left and Paula dug in, he ignored his before finally speaking up.

"When I said that about Val doing anal, I didn't mean to suggest that it was like a huge deal for me."

"Oh," Paula said, chewing daintily. *Don't elaborate. Please don't elaborate.*

"I mean, it's not like I want to do it all the time or ever, even. I'm sorry I brought it up."

"It's okay, Jerry. You were getting something off your chest."

"It's just, I'm not a pervert. I don't want you to think that."

"Jerry, people get up to all kinds of things."

"Sure." He nodded, not looking at her. To her relief, he started eating, spearing a piece of tuna and frowning at it, cross-eyed, before deigning to pop it into his mouth. "You might not believe this, Paula, but I am a very lonely man."

CHAPTER THIRTY-SIX

THE BACK OFFICES OF the auction house were a good deal messier than Rigby expected. Somehow he imagined these art experts to be fastidious types, but the desks were strewn with contracts and invoices and all manner of paperwork, no neater than his own office.

"I don't know when my client will be wanting to sell, but I imagine it will be soon."

The auction house man was a big-framed, gin-blossomed Brit in tweed, who had received Rigby's phone call with almost childish enthusiasm. He examined the photos on Rigby's iPad with bloodshot eyes, bulging and watery. "These are extraordinary. The little Indian girl, but especially the woman. If I'm not mistaken that's Kushik's last wife, and there's no record of his ever having painted her. At least nothing that's ever come onto the market. Provenance?"

"It came to my client's late wife from Mrs. Kushik directly. They both did."

"And your client wishes to remain anonymous."

"He insists."

"And this need for privacy is such that you couldn't even send me these photos of the paintings electronically."

"I'm going to erase them as soon as I leave."

"That need for privacy certainly complicates things. And I will have to make photographs available for potential buyers. But since our buyer will almost certainly be from Russia, there are methods for keeping things under wraps. The auction can be held there, for example, if we can get them out of the country."

"Understood. And I'll set up an LLC for payment."

"Of course you'll still have to notify the IRS. We can't encourage you to do anything illegal or even questionable." He flashed Rigby a lopsided, crooked smile.

"No, of course not."

"When are you returning to Southern California?"

"Tonight, I'm sorry to say. Business to take care of."

The fact was he couldn't afford a decent hotel, not unless he'd brought Beth along, and he was striving at the moment not to complicate that situation any further. The price of a single-day round-trip to SFO had come perilously close to maxing out his Chase Visa, and he didn't want to ask Paula for one of hers because he didn't want her to know how close he was to the line.

"Pity, would have liked to take you for a decent dinner. Well, you needn't make the trip again, I'll come down in a few days and take a look at the canvases in person, and from there we can start making plans for transport, et cetera."

IN THE DISMAL, SEEMINGLY interminable cab ride on the way to the airport—his wounded amour propre would not have survived a trip via courtesy van—he toyed with various ideas for generating short-term cash that didn't involve further pilfering from Haskill's accounts in one way or another, but none of them held any water. When they got to the spot where Candlestick Park once stood, where construction was going on now for some sort of industrial or retail complex, he thought of a ball game he'd seen there ten years earlier, Giants versus Phillies. He thought it was a fucking shame, the lack of respect Americans had for their own past anymore.

"Hey," he said to the cabbie.

"Yes, sir?" the cabbie answered.

Rigby noted the name on the chauffeur's license. "Aziz? Is that it?"

"Yes, sir?" the cabbie said, a little more cautious this time, doubtless afraid that Rigby was going to ask him what he thought about ISIS or Muslim registries.

"You like the Beatles?"

"The Beatles? Sure."

"Did you know the spot we just passed is where they played their very last concert ever?"

"I did indeed. 1966."

"Shame they tore it down, isn't it?"

"The new stadium's much nicer. More convenient."

"You go to a lot of ball games?"

"When I can. My son and daughters are big fans."

"That's good."

He looked out the window again as the 101 curved and wondered about getting season tickets to the Dodgers when the money came through. Start taking the kids again.

THE EARLY EVENING TRAFFIC out of Burbank was monstrous, and he wished he'd stayed over, even though it would have meant bringing Beth along. All the way into Ventura, he wrestled with the notion of calling her, then decided it would be smarter to set his sights on Paula instead, which meant that he had time to stop at the club for a drink.

He had intended to stay for only one, but when he sat down there was a ball game on, Dodgers versus Cards, and still feeling nostalgic from his afternoon's discussion with the cabbie he settled in to watch a few innings. He was halfway through with his second J&B rocks when a familiar waitress sidled up to him. Sweet face, strawberry blond, she was the sort who didn't flirt and so he'd never bothered to learn her name, but there was something he liked about her.

"Mr. Rigby."

"There she is," he said, cursing his memory.

"Long day?"

"Just got back from San Fran."

"Long drive."

"I flew. There and back, same day."

"Ask me about my day."

"All right, how was yours?"

"Better than yesterday. I broke up with my boyfriend."

"Sorry to hear it," he said, though he was mostly confused. He knew perfectly well when a woman was coming on to him and when she wasn't, and this one wasn't. Was she?

"I found out he was sleeping with a married woman."

"Wow, that stinks. Gave him the old heave-ho, did you?"

"You probably know him." She jerked her head in the direction of the golf pro shop, that lovely head of hair bouncing. "Keith. Golf pro."

Keith, fucking a married lady? He wouldn't have thought he had it in him. It made Rigby think a little more highly of him. "Sure, I know him."

"Yeah, I'm not turning him in to the club, even though I probably should."

"Why would the club care?" Then he slapped the side of his head. "Holy shit, he was banging a member?"

"One of his clients. Now, some girls, they'd tell management, get his ass fired and probably blackballed. Not me."

"Huh. Well, you're a good person, I guess."

"Not really. My idea of revenge is to tell her husband his wife is getting fucked by a two-timing, arrested adolescent and people are starting to get wind of it around town. Could be bad for her real estate business."

She patted him on the chest with a mournful smirk and moved away from him. He was trying to figure out precisely how he was getting this wrong. "Wait. Wait a minute."

She turned back to face him. "Sorry, Mr. Rigby."

CHAPTER THIRTY-SEVEN

KEITH WAS NEITHER AS dim-witted nor as boring as Nina had feared, and she found the Town Crier less cringe-inducing than she had on her previous visit. The jukebox was playing at a non-painful volume, and the dirty looks she was still getting from the bartender were less baleful than the last time. They were seated in the same booth as before, and somehow it seemed cleaner this time. At least the table wasn't sticky.

"What I like about you is you're so deadpan," he said. "Like you're watching everybody and judging, but not saying what it is you're thinking."

"Deadpan, huh?"

"Well, yeah. Not grinning all the time when there's nothing to grin about."

She laughed, spoiling, she supposed, the deadpan effect. "It's funny, Mr. Haskill is always telling me I'd be pretty if I smiled. I keep telling him that's the surest way to get me to scowl."

"I like a good scowl on a woman," he said.

Once she'd given him a thumbnail sketch of her life story—childhood in Maine, German-born parents, both academics, both still alive and living in the house she grew up in, two siblings, both married with multiple children, art history degree, teaching jobs until she realized she didn't want to teach or do any more academic work at all—she asked him for his own.

She actually found his story interesting, and when he slowed down, fearful he was boring her, she prompted him to continue. "I don't get why your mom would ever leave a place like this for Kansas."

"My dad. He never wanted to leave Kansas for college, even. And Mom didn't much care where we lived."

"But you ended up here."

"We spent most of our vacations here, and a couple of years they flew me and my sisters out here for the whole summer. I never wanted to live anyplace else."

"Not even LA?"

He shook his head with vigor, eyes closed for emphasis. "Too big and too many people. Too much traffic. Ventura's like Wichita, but with a beach and less shitty weather."

"And you can play golf year-round."

"If you wanted to. I don't love it as much now that I teach it."

"That sounds like me and art history."

He looked over her shoulder toward the door. "Shit."

She turned and spotted Rigby, looking around with a hard-to-read look on his face. It resembled a smile, but fueled by determination and devoid of joy. He spotted them and strode over without stopping at the bar.

"Rigby," Keith said, and Nina prepared an excuse to get them out of the bar in a hurry in case Rigby showed any inclination to join them.

Before replying, Rigby took the back of Keith's head and smashed his face down onto the table. "Don't you fucking 'Rigby' me, you traitorous piece of shit," he said as he yanked Keith out of the booth and onto the floor.

Keith's face was bleeding, and Rigby lifted him up by the front of his shirt before burying his fist in Keith's belly.

"Jesus Christ, Rigby, not again!" the bartender yelled.

"Rigby!" Nina said. "Use your head!"

"You fucked my wife, you piece of shit!" Rigby said, punching him again. Keith went down, and Rigby delivered a vicious kick to his chest. While the bartender went for some fight-stopping implement behind the bar, Nina made haste for the pool table, where she grabbed a cue from the unresisting hands of a muttonchopped player transfixed by the mayhem.

She was too late to stop a second kick to Keith's rib cage, but when the heavy end of the pool cue cracked against Rigby's skull he stopped and spun to face her, left hand to his wounded temple. A drop of blood seeped between his ring and middle finger.

"Stay out of this, Nina. Your boyfriend here fucked my wife."

Then the bartender shouted, and seeing the barrel of a shotgun pointed at his face Rigby raised his hands, looking wounded at the unfairness of it all.

"Goddamnit, Brenda, didn't you hear me say this fart hammer fucked my wife?"

"I give exactly zero shits about that, Rigby. The cops are on their way, and you're eighty-sixed forever this time."

As Rigby backed out, Nina took a wet bar rag, knelt by Keith's side and pressed it to his bleeding forehead. "Did you really fuck his wife, Keith?" she asked.

Keith nodded, miserable. "I did."

"I'd say you've got more balls than brains, then."

In the waiting room at the hospital, she sat looking at her phone and wondering how long decorum required her to stay, how wrong it would be to head for home since the date was technically over. Keith's grandfather had arrived not long after she had, following the ambulance, and had joined him behind the barriers. An admitting nurse had asked Nina if she was the wife, and though she could have said yes, she allowed that they'd been on a first date.

"That's an eventful evening out," the admitting nurse had answered, then directed her to the general waiting area.

She was alone for the moment, this end of Ventura County having apparently experienced a slow evening. The walls were covered with bad paintings of the ocean, and posters featuring ocean-related aphorisms. Printed across a photograph of a beach in the rain was the phrase LIFE ISN'T ABOUT WAITING FOR THE STORM TO PASS . . . IT'S ABOUT LEARNING TO DANCE IN THE RAIN. Another beach, sunny and more tropical-looking than the first, featured a quote from Jimmy Buffett about heaven having a beach attached to it, and Nina began composing uplifting sayings of her own. A BEACH IS THE ONLY PLACE WHERE SAND FEELS GOOD IN YOUR GENITALS. THE OCEAN IS A GIANT GRAVEYARD FOR SAILORS AND FISH.

She looked up and saw Paula coming in from the direction of admissions. When she caught sight of Nina, she looked startled. "What are you doing here?"

"I was there when it happened."

"Have you heard anything?"

"Not yet," Nina said. "Don't worry, though, Rigby won't be up for murder, just felony assault and battery."

Paula sat and leaned back in her chair, head raised to the ceiling, eyes closed, sighing.

Nina couldn't say why exactly, but she wished Paula would leave her alone. "Shouldn't you be down at the county courthouse?"

"What for?"

"Bailing out your husband."

"He can rot in there."

"They say it's always a mistake to leave someone in jail to teach them a lesson. The lockup can be a very dangerous place."

"It seems to me it's in our interests to figure this thing out before we spring him."

"Figure what out?"

"All right, he's found out that . . ." She looked around to reassure herself that they were alone. "That I was having an affair. What's his reaction? Beat the shit out of the guy. What's he going to do to me?"

"Maybe you need to get a restraining order."

She leaned forward, elbows on her knees, hands on her temples. "Can I do that if he hasn't even threatened me?"

A pair of frosted glass doors slid open and Will Seghers walked in. He addressed Nina alone. "Fractured ribs. Two of them, some bad bruising, no concussion, no apparent damage to his internal organs."

"Thank God," Paula said.

He seemed to notice her for the first time. "That meat-head husband of yours is a goddamn menace, you know that?"

She nodded.

"In the name of our shared business interests, Keith's not going to press charges. That doesn't mean the DA won't. But we have to set some rules down."

"Rules," Paula said.

"First off, I'm going to let him know that if anything happens to you, all bets are off. I'll come right out and tell the police and the FBI and whoever else is concerned that I faked that picture so he could steal the real one."

Nina cleared her throat, two dry little clicking sounds. "You do realize that puts us all at risk?"

He stuck a bent, big-knuckled index finger at her. "So did beating the tar out of my grandson."

"Point taken."

"And if he wants to kill me, he can go ahead. It's all on paper, and Keith knows how to get it if he has to. Your husband needs that money, especially now. He's liable to be disbarred after this, if the DA files and gets a conviction."

"I guess the question now is, who bails him out?" Nina said.

"Nobody," Will said.

For a moment it seemed as though one or another of them was about to make a counterargument, but no one did.

CHAPTER THIRTY-EIGHT

HE'D LEFT MESSAGES ON Paula's cell from the pay phone in the holding cell, but he knew she'd have heard by now what he was in there for and he figured the odds of her showing up to bail him out were slim at best. Either she was disgusted at his lack of self-control, horrified at the damage he'd done her boyfriend or furious at the attention he'd drawn to them at the very time they should be avoiding the spotlight.

Then the thought occurred to him that she might be frightened. It was ridiculous, of course. He'd never raised a hand to her in almost twenty years together. Of course, she'd never known of him hurting anyone before, either. And he'd never had a motive to hit her before this, none like this one.

And this led him to the question of what he would say to her. There had to be something really wrong with the marriage if a decent Catholic mother of three was sleeping around. Maybe he wasn't paying enough attention to her in the sack. Maybe he should cut down on the extracurriculars, starting with Beth. Come to think of it, what did he care if Beth liquidated her share of the firm, as long as the Kushiks sold?

He stood up from the long wooden bench and went back to the pay phone.

"Rigby?" Beth said when the operator finally put her through. "What are you doing calling collect?"

"They confiscated my cell. I'm in County."

"County?"

He sighed; she was dense. "County jail. Can you come bail me out?"

"Jail? What the fuck, Rigby?"

"I got in a little dustup with a guy."

"A dustup?"

"I'll explain when you come get me."

WHEN HE HUNG UP, he saw that a tall, skinny prisoner was looking at him from a corner bench. The man had a nose like a hatchet, high-bridged, long and extremely thin, and tiny black eyes. He smiled at Rigby with the right corner of his mouth higher than the left. "I seen you before," he said, slurring, and Rigby assumed he was in on a DUI.

"Doubt it."

"Pretty sure I have." His smile widened into a grin, his teeth long and straight like his nose. He was bald on top with strands of pale red hair grown to comical length at the fringe, most of them now hanging alongside his right temple.

"Thinking of somebody else," he said.

"Don't think so."

"Sounds like you just beat the shit out of somebody."

Rigby didn't say anything, just sat back down on the bench.

"Yeah, that's funny because I was at the Shanty with Ernie Norwin one night, him and a friend of his name of Billy Knox, and Billy was talking about some asshole lawyer who owed him money, and poor Billy's jaw was wired shut because this asshole lawyer"—he drew the last two words out with gusto—"went and broke his jaw. Last time I ever saw Billy before they found him and his girl and old Ernie out in that house in Ojai."

Rigby sat without speaking. There were seven other men in the room, none of whom appeared to be paying any attention to the scarecrow's soliloquy.

"Now, when I heard the cops on TV saying Ernie'd killed the other two and then offed himself, I didn't think that sounded like the Ernie I knew. How about you? You think that same thing?"

"I never heard of any of those people."

"Huh. That's funny, 'cause I'm pretty damn sure I saw you with poor old Ernie. Nice guy, but not too smart."

Now he considered how much of a threat the man might pose once he sobered up. He'd have to get into the day's arrest records and find out his name and address, then check his record. Rigby really didn't want to resort to violence again; he'd found the whole business with Knox very taxing emotionally, and he had better things to think about. He was really starting to regret his attack on Keith at the Town Crier. It would have been a lot smarter to ambush him outside his apartment, or to have avoided a physical confrontation at all. A threat surely would have been enough.

The tall drunk was still talking to him fifteen minutes later when the deputy showed up at the cell door to take him back to processing. Once he'd received his belt, necktie, shoelaces, wallet, keys and cell phone they led him out to the desk where Beth stood, somewhat overdressed for a visit to County and looking not at all pleased.

"Thanks to you, I've had another new experience, Rigby. I never had to bail anyone out before."

He was threading his belt through the loops on his pants. "Always happy to broaden your horizons."

"Don't be a smart-ass." She turned and walked down the hallway without another word. He followed, hoping the silent treatment would continue until they got to his car.

THIS WAS NOT TO be. As soon as she turned her engine over she started to rant. "What the fuck, Rigby, assault and battery? That's a felony."

"Guy won't press charges. I know him."

"Great, at least you're not beating up strangers."

"He's Paula's boyfriend," he said as they left the courthouse parking garage and hit the street. Beth nearly lost control of the car.

"Paula's boyfriend?"

"Jesus, be careful. I'm parked over on Main by Seaward."

"Paula's having an affair?"

"Yes. Did you hear me?"

"I heard you." She shook her head. "This is perfect. Gives you an excuse to leave her."

"Yeah, about that. This may not be an ideal time to be making big changes, Beth."

She let out a chuckle that struck Rigby as evil. "Don't think you're getting out of this that easy."

"I'm serious."

She stared straight ahead down Telephone Road. After half a mile of silence she spoke, her voice low and level. "That law firm of yours is costing me money. I might have to liquidate my share. Think you can survive with one client?"

On another night he might have reverted to his usual, effortlessly ass-rimming persona, might have ended up at her house or at least in a hotel room, but tonight it just wasn't in him. "I'll manage."

She pulled the car over to the side of the road. "Get out."

"Jesus, Beth."

"Get out of this vehicle right the fuck now."

"Baby, this is a long way from my car."

"Don't call me baby. Get out."

It wasn't an ideal situation, but it wasn't the night's low point. He unbuckled, opened the door and stepped out. "I'll talk to you tomorrow."

"You'll talk to my lawyer. Who is no longer you, in case you hadn't figured that out."

She drove off, and he supposed he was grateful not to have to listen to her on the long walk to where his car was parked. He took the necktie out of his pocket and draped it around his throat. It was a loud one, seafoam green and coral paisley, an old anniversary gift from Paula, and something had told him that morning that it would appeal to the type of artsy asshole who'd run an auction house, a man who, as it happened, had himself shown up in shirtsleeves with no tie at all.

HE HAD JUST ABOUT reached the Town Crier when he spotted Bobby Theele trying to parallel park a '90s model Cadillac across the street, efforts comical enough to make him stop and linger. He crunched the bumpers of the cars in front of and behind him, though not grievously, and after landing the front-right tire on the sidewalk for the third time, Bobby gave up and put it into park. Reeling, he crossed Main and raised his bushy eyebrows at the sight of Rigby.

"Thurston Howell the third, in person," he roared into the night. "Just in time to buy me a drink in my own establishment."

"I'm not welcome in there anymore, Bobby, I'm eighty-sixed for life."

"Bullshit, I already rescinded that."

"Happened again tonight."

Bobby stepped gingerly out of the gutter onto the sidewalk, arms akimbo for balance. "Jesus." He held onto Rigby's shoulder and managed to stay upright. "Well, I'm the only one with any say on permanent eighty-six or not. Come on in."

Bobby opened up the big door and gestured for Rigby to precede him, and all at once it sounded like fun, so he went on in. Bobby followed and they took seats at the bar. Looking around he didn't see anyone he remembered from earlier in the evening except for Brenda, currently occupied at the other end of the bar with a small cluster of what looked to Rigby like underage boys. Of course he hadn't really been paying much attention to the rest of the bar's clientele during his previous visit, but nobody looked alarmed at the sight of him.

"Look at her," Bobby said. "You'd think I paid her to flirt. Two customers walk in the door, and she's standing over there talking, doesn't even look up." She was leaning with her elbows on the bar, hands clasped under her chin and looking charmed by whatever the wispy-mustached fellow on the other side of it was saying to her. Bobby cupped his hands around his mouth.

"Wench!" he shouted, and she turned to face him, eyes narrowed. "We need whisky."

She started to reach for a glass when she registered Rigby's presence. Her hands went to her hips, then she lifted her right hand and pointed straight at his face. "Of all the sets of balls I ever saw in my life. I eighty-sixed you for life not four hours ago and here you waltz back in like it never happened."

"I rescinded it," Bobby said.

She turned her condemnatory index finger to Bobby. "And you. You're shit-faced. You get not one thimbleful."

"May I remind you who signs your paycheck?"

"Not much longer if this keeps up, Bobby. You know what this shitbird did? He beat up another customer, bad enough this time that we had cops and an ambulance. Which in my opinion is bad for business. So you can wait around for a cab if you want, but no sauce for you, and this cocksucker has to leave this second or I'll walk out that door right now."

Bobby looked stricken, and Rigby guessed that this was the most intense display of piss and vinegar to which Brenda had ever treated the old boy. Bobby stood and stuck his chin out in a poor semblance of proud defiance. "All right, Thirsty, boy, let's go. I can tell we're not wanted."

As they headed for the door, the crowd watching with puzzlement, Brenda called out. "And if you decide to let that asshole back in here I'm done and I mean it."

VISIBLY CHASTENED, BOBBY STUCK his hands in his pants pockets. "Guess you're going to have to find another place to go from now on."

"That's okay. Want a ride somewhere? I'm parked just a couple blocks away. Plus I'm sober."

"You beat up a guy sober?"

"Found out he was fucking my wife."

Bobby shrugged, as if he found it hard to understand that as a motivator for powerful emotions. "If I found out somebody was fucking Constance I'd hire a private eye to get pictures, then divorce her and keep all the assets."

"Divorce law doesn't work that way anymore, Bobby."

"Ah, it'd still be an excuse to get her off my fucking back."

"I can't get a divorce."

"Sure you can."

"I'm Catholic."

"Join the Episcopalians. Same thing, but you can get a divorce."

"Not quite."

"All right. So how do you settle things, now you know she's been messing around?"

"I haven't figured it out yet. I guess we'll just agree she won't do it anymore." Hearing himself say it out loud, he knew how weak that sounded.

CHAPTER THIRTY-NINE

"HEY, IRENE, SOME GUY in lockup wants to talk to someone in Homicide. Says it's about the Magda Schuller thing."

She didn't look up from her unfinished report, which she needed to finish before her shift ended in half an hour. "Case is closed, Chuck."

"No, it's not."

"Might as well be. Norwin killed Knox and Schuller, came back a few days later and killed himself."

He brushed his hand on the back of his head. She could almost hear the ruffling of the bristles, and she didn't like the way he was looking at her, like she was slacking off on a case because of her disapproval of the victims' way of life. It was true, but Chuck was a prig and a pain in the ass and she didn't need any more of his shit.

"Guy says he knows something. I'll talk to him myself."

She stood up. Shit, with her luck, he'd catch a break and solve her case and make her look like an asshole in the process. "All right, get him into an interrogation room. I'll be there in five."

A SULLEN, LIPLESS, BUTTON-NOSED deputy buzzed her into the interrogation room and went to stand behind the prisoner, who was seated with his left wrist cuffed to the leg of the old formica-topped table before him. He grinned with a mouthful of jagged, crooked teeth, but they looked damaged by hard living and lack of dental care rather than meth; she pegged him for a boozer rather than a tweaker. He was looking at her as though they were going to be the best of friends, and it would have taken more effort than she was capable of offering to fake the slightest friendliness in return. That might work to her advantage or not, but it had been a long day and she wanted to learn whatever this reprobate had to impart and then finish her report and get home to her dogs. She sat down, arms crossed, and opened his file.

"Mr. Imhoff, I'm Lieutenant Ortega. Heard you might know something about an ongoing investigation."

"Yeah, I just might." He gave her a slow, portent-laden nod, and she fought the temptation to roll her eyes.

"Shoot."

"Whoa, I'm not saying I'll give it up for free."

"You're not getting paid."

"I didn't say anything about money. I just want a little consideration."

"Receipt of stolen goods and violation of probation. And looking at the rest of your jacket . . ." She flipped through the file folder and put it down on the table. "You'd have to come up with something pretty spectacular for me to talk to the county attorney on your behalf."

"Call him in, then."

"I'll call her in when I've heard your story and if it's of use to me in my investigation."

"Man. There goes my incentive. You cop types don't have much understanding of human nature."

"Sure we do. And human nature is such that if I promised you something and what you gave me in return was worthless, I'd be a fool. So if you want a little consideration from the sheriff's department, you're going to have to pony up."

His smile was gone, and his tiny, porcine eyes glistened with tears at the unfairness of it. According to his intake report, his BAC had been at .18 when they'd brought him in. "All right. A guy in holding with me. Big muscly guy, dressed too nice for County, if you see what I mean."

"Go on."

"Well, I've seen this guy before. He's trying to call some woman on the pay phone, collect, but she won't pick up. Takes me a few minutes to figure out where I know him from. And then it hits me. You know the Shanty?"

"On East Main."

"That's the one. I knew Ernie Norwin there, and Billy Knox a little bit, too. Not the girl so much, met her maybe once or twice, but she didn't really fit in there."

"Okay."

"So this big muscleman, I remember seeing him in there one night talking to Ernie, real serious. This is maybe a week before Billy shows up with his jaw broken. You following me?"

"Uh-huh."

"And not long after that Billy goes missing along with the girl. Ernie mopes around for a few days, missing his buddy."

"More like feeling guilty for having killed him and Schuller."

"And then Ernie disappears."

She nodded, careful not to seem encouraging.

"So listen, I know you're thinking Ernie's your man, but I'm thinking it's Mr. Charles Atlas from holding tonight."

"The fact that you saw him talking to Ernie Norwin means nothing unless you heard what they were talking about."

"How's this, then? When Billy showed up back at the Shanty with his broken jaw, he was talking about how some rich lawyer sucker-punched him."

She sat up, trying not to seem excited at the new information. "All right, Mr. Imhoff, your information is being logged and noted, and if it proves useful we'll talk some more and I'll put in a good word with the county attorney's office."

His jaw hung open. "I was hoping I'd get out of here tonight."

"If you can make bail, that's a possibility."

"I meant my story in lieu of bail."

"Come on, Stewart. You go by Stew?"

He nodded.

"Come on, Stew. You know better than that." She nodded to the deputy. "Back to holding."

SHE CHECKED THE EVENING'S intake reports and found a record for an attorney named Rigby, booked for assault and battery. Her breath started coming a bit faster. Home address in the hills. She looked it up on Google Earth and found what looked like at least a million-dollar house. Then she asked herself what a guy like that might be doing mixed up with a couple of tweakers like Ernie Norwin and Billy Knox, if indeed he was. Released on bond, put up by a woman giving a different home address.

CHAPTER FORTY

JERRY LAY IN THE dark, staring at the ceiling of his uncle's guest room, completely at a loss. It was close to 2 A.M., which made it almost 4 A.M. by his body clock.

The call had come after he and Paula had come back from LA that afternoon. He'd been sitting in an Adirondack chair on his uncle's patio. It was the fifth call from that St. Louis number in two days, and feeling bold, or fatalistic, he'd answered. "Mr. Haskill? This is Peter Bolling down at Community Federal. How are you doing this afternoon?"

Though he'd known it would be the bank, Jerry's sphincter had clenched nonetheless. "I'm just fine, Mr. Bolling."

"I left several messages, I was worried something might be the matter."

"I'm just, I'm very busy at the moment and I didn't recognize the number, and I never pick up if I don't know the number. Too many scammers, if you know what I mean."

"Sure I do. I get those all the time myself. Mr. Haskill, I've been assigned your various accounts by our branch manager."

"What happened to Nadia?"

"Nadia moved to our branch in Westport."

"Oh."

"I'm looking at your paperwork here, and to be honest with you, Nadia should have taken steps some months ago.

I'd like to sit down with you at your earliest opportunity and talk about our options, which I'm sorry to say are not many. Any way you could make it in this afternoon?"

"I'm in California at the moment."

"I see."

"It's my uncle, he's dying, and I'm here to be with him and help wrap things up. I was planning on getting together with Nadia when I got back, discussing how to invest the inheritance, et cetera. After, obviously, getting my accounts in order. The mortgage first and foremost, obviously. And there'll be the matter of a valuable painting I'll have to sell. My uncle keeps it in a vault in Beverly Hills."

"Of course," Mr. Bolling had said, unconvinced.

"So would it be all right if I came in as soon as I get back to St. Louis?"

"When do you anticipate being back?"

"That all depends on my uncle."

"If you're back by, say, end of next week?"

"Oh, I'd say I will be. The old boy's got one foot in the grave and the other on a banana peel." He'd forced a chuckle. "If not I'll give you a call."

"I really want to work this out with you, Mr. Haskill, but we can't keep on as before. Nadia really did cross a few lines she shouldn't have in your case."

HE HADN'T STOPPED THINKING about it since. This was bad. Nadia had always felt sorry for him, and he'd always been able to talk her into another delay or renegotiation, and the fact that she'd been reassigned without even warning him filled him with terror. This Bolling was no doubt some sort of financial Javert who would take the whole messy situation apart and destroy him with glee. The worst part was that his lie about Uncle Glenn had been true until the damned nephrologist had come and revived him. And now he was going to have to go home and face foreclosure and bankruptcy and general ruination.

IT MADE HIS STOMACH hurt, and he'd skipped dinner. He tried to call Paula Rigby to talk it out, but she didn't pick up, and probably that was good. He didn't want her to know how close to the edge he was. He didn't want Rigby to know, and certainly not his uncle, who had made clear on numerous occasions his disappointment at Jerry's fecklessness, at his having squandered everything. He could hear the old man's scolding, contemptuous voice, just like the time he'd had to fold the scooter dealership, and the coffee roastery after that. And there he lay sleeping, just down the hall, with only the gin-blossomed nurse for company. Or protection.

CHAPTER FORTY-ONE

WHEN THEY REACHED RIGBY'S SUV, Bobby had some difficulty getting in, and Rigby wondered about the wisdom of getting him any drunker, but he wanted somebody to bounce this off of. "How about the Shanty?"

"Sure," Bobby said. "It's a shithole, but why not."

They drove north on Main, Bobby giving a running commentary on all the failed businesses that had once filled the empty storefronts. "This stretch of Main's like the small-business graveyard. Hey, remember twenty years back, there was a coffin store up the street, little bit farther than this? Fucking showroom, like they were selling furniture. Which I guess coffins are, kind of."

"That was before I got here."

"That's right, you're a kid. So this straying wife of yours, she some kind of bored housewife banging the plumber, or she work?"

It's because he's old that he feels free to say any goddamn thing that pops into his head, not because he's plastered. Rigby could think of any number of people he would have punched for talking about his wife that way, but somehow coming from Bobby Theele, it didn't bother him at all.

"Hold on." He pulled over to the curb and made a U-turn, then headed south.

"Hey, Thirsty, Shanty's the other way."

"Just want to show you something." He stopped across the street from one of Paula's bus benches, illuminated by the orange haze of a streetlamp. "That's her on the bench."

Bobby squinted at the picture. It was a good one. She looked sexy but professional, and looking at it gave Rigby the unaccustomed urge to cry.

"Well, shit, now I can understand your desire to kill the guy. Listen up, though, how's about we turn back around and get a drop to drink?"

GOING BACK TO THE Shanty was a risky move, but he needed to figure out what to do about that stick insect back at the holding cell, and he figured the ambience might stimulate his thought processes. When he'd gone in to meet Ernie Norwin they'd sat at a corner table, occupied now by a couple in their forties holding hands and discussing something very earnestly, the male deeply distressed and the female consoling but firm. He had the feeling he knew the woman from somewhere; she was heavier than he guessed she'd like to be, but to Rigby's mind she was a very pleasing size. Not the kind of woman he'd necessarily want on his arm at a social function, but one he'd love to slap bellies with. Then she came into focus; she was a paralegal who'd started working at the old firm just before he and Britt had left. Did she recognize him? She hadn't looked in the direction of the bar that he'd seen, but here was a perfect example of why coming here was a bad idea.

"You sure got quiet all of a sudden, Thirsty."

"Got a lot on my mind."

"Drink your drink, then. You got a lot of catching up to do."

Rigby tossed back his Jack and Coke. They had better brands on the shelf, but he'd said to himself walking in that as long as he was in a dive he ought to drink accordingly. He held up the empty glass and twirled his index finger in a circle. In response the bartender made a sound like mucus going through a dog's throat and made his drink without any other acknowledgment.

"You know, when they built this place it was one of the best in town. Live music every night. Now it's just a good place to get laid or stabbed."

"I'll pass on both."

"Ventura was a lot livelier before the 101 came through. Route 66, you had to drive through town, not around it. S'why we have all those motels. Used to be full of families traveling through. Now they're all halfway houses."

"I've had clients lived in those motels. Probably a few of them come in here."

"I bet you're the first man been in here in a year in a coat and tie," Bobby said.

Rigby fingered the tip of the thick end of his necktie. "Don't know why I put this goddamn thing back on after they let me out."

"That's kind of a loud one for a day in court."

The bartender came over with the next round and left without speaking, plainly seething with resentment toward the two of them and, in fact, toward everyone in the bar. Rigby assumed that this was his habitual state.

"I wasn't in court. Went upstate this morning to negotiate a deal, wanted to look sharp. Got back tonight, found out my wife was fucking another guy, beat said guy up, went to jail, girlfriend bailed me out and dumped me."

"Girlfriend." He raised an eyebrow and reared his head back.

"Mistress. You like that better?"

"Semantics. All's I'm saying is maybe that's why she strayed."

"Oh, no, huh-uh. She doesn't know about this—at least she didn't until real recently."

"So you say." He jerked his head in the bartender's direction. "Bartender looks like Jack Elam without the walleye, don't he."

Rigby studied the man, staring now with a child's studied petulance at the floor. He had a remarkably round head, hair heavy and curly on the sides and quite sparse up top, and big, wide-set eyes with black, caterpillar brows. "Who's Jack Elam?"

"Ah, you kids, you don't know shit anymore."

AFTER HE DROPPED BOBBY off at his house—nobly ignoring the old man's demands to be deposited at his car—he started to drive home, then reconsidered. Paula had to know what had happened by now, and he didn't want to hash the thing out with her tonight. Anything he had to say to her would be better expressed after a night's sleep. The problem was he didn't have a working credit card, so a hotel was out of the question, and Beth wasn't about to let him in.

So he headed for the office, where he could choose between the couch or the meager remainder of his stash of coke. It was two-thirty in the morning, and he tried to drop off on the couch, but with his feet dangling over the edge and his head resting on the thinly upholstered arm he gave up inside of twenty minutes and opened the office safe. There was less in the envelope than he'd expected; he must have had a bigger taste than he remembered the night he killed Ernie. But there was enough to keep him awake, to keep his mind churning. He dwelt on Paula for a few minutes, but he'd already discharged that anger in what he now realized had been quite a satisfying manner, and he considered now what effect the beating he'd administered might have on the business relationship. Probably not a good one.

He took another hit, just to keep the clarity of focus he'd achieved. Things were starting to come together in his mind. There was always a way out if you concentrated hard enough.

All right, Paula was going to be mad, and Will definitely wouldn't appreciate his grandson's pummeling. Nina would see it for what Rigby could now see that it was: a serious breach of esprit de corps and an unnecessary and dangerous calling of attention to their group. But the amount of money involved was sufficient, he hoped, to preclude any defections.

The thing had to go down soon, though, especially if Beth was serious about pulling out her share of equity in the firm. The buyers could be lined up in a matter of days. The only thing keeping the process from moving forward was Glenn Haskill's stubborn failure to succumb to the various illnesses that the doctors had predicted would have him underground by now.

What if Glenn lasted another six months? A year? Two . . . Jesus. Who knew, the old bastard might make it to a hundred, in which case Rigby would need a prison furlough to attend the funeral. In the best-case scenario, he'd just lose his license to practice law.

He took another little toot, and it was as though a light had come on, flooding the inside of his skull. There'd been a phrase the vet's assistant used when they'd put the kids' cat Tubby down the year before. They weren't putting him to sleep, they were helping the poor sick old feline over the Rainbow Bridge.

I have to help Glenn cross the Rainbow Bridge.

It was an awful realization, that his own survival depended

upon the murder of his good friend and valued client, but the fact was, he'd be doing the poor sick son of a bitch a favor. What could he look forward to but repeated hospital stays and health crises and endless conversations about starlets fucked long ago and the occasional dinner at Arnoldi's? Death would be a blessing.

The alarm code was Evvie's birthday backward. Jerry would be there, asleep in the guest room. So would Nina, in her little room downstairs. He could get past either one of them without a sound. The presence of the nurse was the problem, but lately the alcoholic with the pale, thin red hair had been getting the night shift, and Rigby knew she had a way of falling asleep in her chair when she was supposed to be keeping an eye on his oxygen levels. Glenn had mentioned it; several times he'd awakened to the sound of her snoring. He hadn't wanted her fired, though, because he thought that, given her tendency toward insobriety, he might have a shot at one last fling. He had in fact gone over the prospect with Rigby in nauseating detail.

"How do I arrange this so she can't sue me if she doesn't bite?" he'd asked.

"There's always that risk, Glenn," Rigby had said. "You'll just have to use your usual charm and finesse."

CHAPTER FORTY-TWO

IT WAS ALMOST THREE in the morning. The unanticipated adrenaline rush of the early evening had killed Nina's urge to fall asleep, and she sat in her little room reading a history of the Boer War by the light of her bedside lamp. Haskill was still unaware of Rigby's arrest, as was the nephew, but word would be out before long. The old man wouldn't much care—he'd probably think it was funny—but Jerry might pay closer attention, might even be smart enough to look into the relationships among the assorted players involved, particularly if Rigby's motive became public record.

She started at the sound of a floorboard creaking above her head. Someone was walking so slowly, it was plain that they were either trying hard not to be detected or were extremely infirm. She turned out the lamp and quietly moved to the door. Upstairs, the floorboards griped at a glacial but clearly deliberate rate. Barefoot, she mounted the back staircase and, arriving at the top, peeked around the corner. There she was treated to the sight of a barefoot Jerry Haskill tiptoeing like a cartoon burglar toward his uncle's room.

Still unaware of Nina's presence, Jerry opened the door with exquisite care and peered inside. Was the redheaded alkie nurse awake? Was he there to seduce the woman?

Surely not, but who knew with an oddball like Jerry. Maybe he was going to wake his uncle and talk about the Kushik?

She was going to be very fucking glad when this was all over with, Haskill in the ground, the paintings sold, the money in her bank account. Working with these basket cases was taking its toll on her equilibrium.

CHAPTER FORTY-THREE

GLENN AWOKE FROM AN exquisite dream about an up-and-coming starlet he once cast as a stewardess in an episode of *Flyboys*. In the dream it was now, more or less, but she was still the nubile young thing he'd cornholed on his office couch in 1966. She was asking him if he wanted her to take the uniform off or leave it on when he awoke to the sound of the nurse snoring, a long, low, wet intake of air followed twenty or so seconds later by a sharp, whistling exhalation.

"Wake up," he said, his voice a quiet hiss unlikely to stir anyone as deep in her cups as Myrna was. He nearly added an obscene epithet but, mindful of his hopes at one last August–December liaison, held his tongue. "You ruined the best dream I've had in ten years."

The snoring continued. He closed his eyes and willed himself back to sleep, focusing on images of the actress in a mid-sixties United Airlines stewardess uniform. Then he tried to think of her name. She'd gone on to do small roles in *Star Trek* and, the next year, *Batman*, and he'd thought she might actually make it, but she hadn't. At least he had the glorious memory of that messy afternoon in the office.

Despite the snoring, which he was blocking out of his consciousness with some success, he found himself becoming aroused. Hot diggety dog! Ninety-five years old and still the occasional hard-on, unbidden, pharmaceutically speaking, appeared in his shorts like a surprise package in the mail. Eyes still shut, his right hand snuck under the covers and just as he grasped his pecker her name came to him.

Kirstin! Blond, big-eyed, busty Kirstin!

And TV producer or no, there weren't too many girls back then who'd go for any kind of back-door action. He was stroking and transported back to that day, only now she was wearing that stewardess uniform, skirt hiked up around her hips, moaning and carrying on, and somehow the sound of the nurse's snoring added to the experience. When he came it didn't take long, and he was surprised at the amount of ejaculate that landed on his belly.

He barely noted the creaking of the bedroom door, and there was a smile on his face when one of the pillows was yanked from beneath his head, and he opened his eyes for just a second to see his nephew holding it, then placing it firmly over his face.

Goddamn it. He tried to scream, to wake the sleeping sot in the chair by the window, but the pillow covered his face tightly, and the sound that came out was feeble and tiny. *That tosspot just lost her job, I don't care how badly I wanted to fuck her before this!*

It was only then that he thought to be outraged at Jerry. The little bastard! He screamed it, through the pillow, his heart racing, his thin ejaculate cold on his belly:

I should have pulled out of your rotten mother!

He was about to scream at Jerry that he was hereby disinherited, and he made a mental note to call Rigby in the morning to arrange it, and then everything got very quiet.

CHAPTER FORTY-FOUR

AN HOUR LATER, JERRY sat on the edge of his bed, weeping at a childhood memory of Uncle Glenn taking him to the set of *Submarine Patrol* and introducing him to that episode's guest star, James Gregory. On another occasion he'd been allowed on the set of *You Can't Cheat Fate*, a series for which his uncle had had high hopes, but which had been canceled after only six episodes. Nonetheless, he had met Julie Newmar—the Catwoman herself!—playing a nightclub singer accused in a murder-for-hire plot.

And another Southern California visit at seventeen, when Uncle Glenn had taken him to a fancy apartment in Beverly Hills and introduced him to a beautiful woman whom Jerry took at first for an actress. She was beautiful and dressed in a way that suggested money and breeding, and he'd found himself fixated on her nylon-clad knees while she and his uncle discussed something he could no longer remember.

And then his uncle had risen and announced his departure, and Jerry had risen as well, and his uncle and the woman laughed and the woman—her name was Victoria—held him back and said, "Not so fast. He'll be back to get you later." And then she laughed and his uncle left and it was just like that Bobby Goldsboro song about getting deflowered by a beautiful older lady. He was as ridiculously grateful to Uncle Glenn tonight for that afternoon as he had been at the time.

Uncle Glenn treated him with contempt occasionally, it was true, but on the whole he had always shown Jerry kindness, investing in numerous long-shot investments and helping keep the coffee roastery afloat for a while after the recession hit. Good God, what had he just done?

CHAPTER FORTY-FIVE

SHE WAS SITTING AT the kitchen table with the lights off, contemplating the jacaranda in the glow of the yard lights and considering her best course of action, when she saw a figure creeping through the yard and then lurking for a minute before taking off his shoes at the kitchen door, then punching in the alarm code and slipping inside. He was standing next to the door letting his eyes adjust to the dim light when she spoke.

"Rigby," she said, and his yelp was so high-pitched she laughed. "It's Nina."

He leaned forward, squinting. "What the fuck, you just about gave me a heart attack. What are you doing up?"

"How about I ask the questions."

"I know, it's late."

"Four A.M., almost. You could say it's early."

"I came by to talk to Glenn."

She understood now that a considerable chunk of Rigby's ability to con resided in his face; in the dark, he didn't seem like a very good liar. "At four in the morning."

"I wanted to tell him about last night before he heard someone else's version."

"That's not happening. The poor nurse just got him back to sleep, he was having some kind of manic episode. Dreamed he was fucking Jane Russell, woke up screaming."

Shit. This wasn't happening tonight, was it? "I don't know who that is."

"Doesn't matter. Haskill does. So why don't you piss off and come back in the morning. I'll make sure you're the one who tells him all about it."

He stood there for a moment, and she had the impression he was about to propose something to her, but then he turned and opened the door back up. "Fair enough. I'm sorry, Nina, I know I really fucked up tonight."

Once again, her inability to see his face made him sound less sincere than usual, and she didn't bother to fake it herself when she answered. "Yeah, I'd say you did. Go home and get some sleep."

"Can't really go home tonight."

"Well, as the saying goes, you don't have to go home, but you can't stay here."

He walked through the yard with his hands in his pockets, looking so pathetic she almost rejected the ideas that were forming. But the more she rolled over the scenario in her head, the more sense it made. All the neighbors' houses had exterior lights and video surveillance. It would be a simple matter to establish Rigby's presence here tonight, if someone wanted to prove it.

CHAPTER FORTY-SIX

ORTEGA HAD BEEN IN the office since seven-fifteen, studying the witness statements, the autopsy reports and any and all court records involving the victims. It was eleven-thirty when she came across it: Rigby had represented Ernest Norwin when his ex-wife tried to garnish his wages over delinquent child support payments. It wasn't much, but it was a direct link between suspect and victim and it supported Imhoff's claim of seeing them together, and if the captain would just okay a few days of digging, she might have enough to take the county attorney.

The captain waved her in without speaking and indicated the chair across from his desk. His vitreous were red and she had an idea he might be hungover, and when he leaned back he folded his arms across his chest in a manner that did not inspire confidence in his open-mindedness or good cheer.

"I've got something on the Knox-Norwin-Schuller case."

He closed his eyes and pressed the tips of his fingers to their inner corners, and when he spoke he sounded physically pained. "The case is closed, Lieutenant. The county's official position is that Ernie Norwin killed his two friends and at some later date killed himself at the same locale."

"I don't believe that."

He leaned forward and opened his eyes. "I'm not sure I

do, but barring some spectacular revelation I'm not inclined to waste any more man-hours on it."

"I have a witness."

He raised an eyebrow. "To the murders?"

"Okay, no, but he saw my suspect with Ernie Norwin at the Shanty, and earlier he'd heard Billy Knox talking about a lawyer who'd busted his jaw over a debt."

The captain was giving her the look he gave cops he considered to be wasting his or the department's time, a dubious half-smirk with his left eye asquint. "Heard a dead man talking about a lawyer. That'll be a fun moment at trial, when the whole defense table jumps up at once and yells, 'Objection!'"

"This lawyer also represented Ernie Norwin on a child support beef."

The captain shook his head and let loose with a nasty rasp of a chuckle. "Ortega, you know better than this. If these people were upstanding, taxpaying citizens and there was any sort of pressure whatsoever, I'd say sure, look into this lawyer. Or if you had something more solid to show."

Heading down the corridor toward the garage, it felt as though the only thing that would make her feel better was the opportunity to punch someone in the face. She'd skipped breakfast, and if she didn't get some food into her soon she was liable to do just that, so she drove downtown and sat at the counter at the coffee shop outside the Best Western. The Santa Barbara NBC affiliate's noon newscast was just coming on as her BLT arrived, the anchor breathlessly promising something that would turn the community on its ear. MURDER IN MONTECITO, read the graphic over an image of a stately, early-twentieth-century mansion. She had just taken her first bite and was only three bites in when she almost inhaled it at the sight of the presumed perpetrator being led away from the house in cuffs.

Sullen and cunning, he looked like he'd kill for the price of a pack of cigarettes. VENTURA ATTORNEY HELD WITHOUT BAIL, the next caption read, and Rigby's face was replaced by that of a humorless thirtyish woman.

NINA NORDMANN, WITNESS

"I heard noises, something like a struggle, and then it stopped, and when I looked out the window I saw Mr. Rigby leaving out the front door. Then this morning I found Mr. Haskill. We all thought it was a heart attack, he was ninety-six, but then I saw the mustache print on the pillow and I knew he'd been smothered. That's when I called the sheriff's department."

A short montage of old TV shows replaced the woman, and Ortega resumed chewing. Fucking Santa Barbara got him. No point pursuing any of this anyway, but at least she could hold it over the captain that she'd been right about this character.

CHAPTER FORTY-SEVEN

IN CONTRAST TO THE one before, with Haskill's cremation and a brief, grim visit to Rigby in the Santa Barbara County jail during which Paula informed him that she would be unable and for that matter unwilling to make his bail, this day was starting on a note of fun. She was dealing with business directly, and the waiting was over.

When she tapped on the window of the kitchen door of the Montecito house, Jerry was sitting at the table in one of Glenn's old silk bathrobes the old man used to think made him look like his idol and putative buddy Hugh Hefner. Jerry, a good seventy pounds heavier than his late uncle, gave off more of an injured-swine-wrapped-in-a-plastic-tarp vibe, and his vulnerable look of hope at the sight of her provoked a tiny pang of empathy, easy to ignore. Nina opened the door and directed her to a seat and poured her a cup of coffee.

The house felt now as though it had sat empty for decades. Funny how she'd never noticed while Glenn was alive how musty and decrepit it had become. The wallpaper—slender, vertical white and canary-yellow stripes—was peeling at the borders, and nicotine stained the ceiling a dark, rusty color around the smoke alarm, though Paula knew for a fact that Glenn and Evvie had both quit cigarettes around the time Reagan was elected. "How are you holding up, Jerry?" she asked.

Bashful, Jerry looked down at his own coffee cup. "Okay, considering."

Nina sat between them. "All right, Jerry, down to business."

Jerry was confused. He looked first to Nina and, seeing no sign of sympathy, turned to Paula. She took his hands in hers across the small table and gave him a kindly nod and squeeze. The motor of the refrigerator, an avocado relic from the late seventies, cycled on, producing the only sound in the kitchen for a few seconds until Nina spoke.

"Jerry, it was a good try. If I hadn't been awake, you might have pulled it off."

He looked baffled and then terrified. Paula clasped his hands harder. "Ssshhh," she said.

"I told the police about seeing Rigby here last night," Nina said. "That will be corroborated by the security cameras, but it's important that I saw him come here."

Jerry nodded, his mouth open. More than ever he looked to Paula like an overgrown, prepubescent boy.

"I'll be testifying under oath when this thing gets to trial, whether the defendant is you or Rigby. I'm perfectly happy to leave out the part where I sent him away without ever letting him in. Also the part where I heard a ruckus in your uncle's room and saw you coming out." From her bag beneath the table she pulled a SIM card, which she held between thumb and forefinger. "And I'll leave this in my safe-deposit box."

"There was a camera?" Jerry said.

"The only one from the old security system that still worked. I think the old boy liked to film himself with call girls, who knows. Anyway, don't worry, I disconnected it and the cops have no idea it was ever there." She waggled the SIM card. "You want this copy as a goodwill gesture?"

Wide-eyed, he shook his head no. This gambit had been

a risk; there had never been a camera, but Nina was sure he wouldn't ever have the stomach to watch himself snuffing out his uncle's lights.

"But in order for me to perjure myself, Paula and I are going to need some things from you."

The two of them proceeded to explain to him how it was going to be. He would make a significant cash investment in Paula's brand-new real estate firm, and although the county attorney was certain to identify the funds Rigby embezzled from Haskill's accounts as a motive for murder, Jerry would privately consider it a loan and forgive it. Nina would receive, as she and Jerry would both recall had been Haskill's fervent but unwritten wish, the property, house and its furnishings. The "Kushik"—the third one, the one Jerry had seen—would go as planned to Haskill's alma mater in St. Louis. This left Jerry, as Nina figured it, close to three million dollars in cash and securities plus Haskill's ownership stakes in a dozen old television shows, half of which were still generating revenue.

"This is blackmail," he said.

Paula smiled tenderly and again she squeezed his hands, slick and cold now with sweat. "Sweetie, you understand that a murderer can't inherit from his victim, right? We're doing you a favor."

Nina nodded. "It's true, you're getting a hell of a deal here, Jer. Now I've taken the liberty of speaking to a lawyer who'd be happy to represent the estate, given that the original counsel is incarcerated. We're meeting at his office on State at one P.M. for you to sign some papers."

He sat there for a minute with his mouth hanging open and his eyes wet, then shrugged and drank the remnants of his cold coffee. "I guess it could be worse."

NOW THEIR FLIGHT WAS descending into SFO, the paintings in the cargo hold below. A brief conversation with the art dealer had established that he was delighted to be dealing with the two of them instead of Rigby, whose legal troubles didn't interest him any more than they would his Russian clientele. They were booked into the St. Regis for three nights, Danny was in charge of the house and his sisters while she was gone—their father's situation had been explained to them but not in any detail, and with the strong implication that he was innocent and would surely be exonerated—and as the day progressed, she found that she liked Nina better and better. She was exchanging noncommittal texts with Keith and honestly didn't much care how things went with him. Either way was fine. The future was hers to call, and once they'd split the money from the picture, she could take him or leave him.

"Where do you want to get dinner?" Nina asked.

"I don't know, someplace corny in North Beach?"

"Fuck that, that's for tourists. We're getting something expensive tonight."

She nodded. Sounded good to her.

EPILOGUE

"JESUS, RIGBY, LOOK AT you, are you juicing?"

He looked around, then back across the table at Paula and shushed her. "Shut the fuck up. That shit's strictly contraband in here."

"You are. My God, you're huge."

"Not much for a guy to do in here but lift."

"I guess not."

"That and read. I volunteer at the library, too. Keep my commissary account full doing legal work for the other guys."

"You're disbarred. Couldn't that land you in trouble?"

He gestured around the visitation room. "Worse than twenty-five to life?"

"Right."

"Anyway, my legal judgment's as good right now as it was when I was licensed."

She smirked but didn't comment.

"You look good, Paula." She did, too, hair a little longer than had been her habit over the years, complexion flushed and clear. Gone was the anxious look to which he'd become accustomed without ever quite noticing. "Kids okay?"

"They're good. Girls are getting used to the new school."

"Notice you didn't bring 'em."

"They'll come, give them time."

"So I was talking to the priest the other day. He's a great guy, grew up in Sierra Leone. I was complaining about . . ." He lowered his voice. "I was confessing, actually, about masturbation."

"I don't need to hear about that, Rigby."

"No, listen. I said, 'Father, I'm doing it twice a day, three times. I know it's wrong, but I'm not going to go queer just because I'm incarcerated.' You know me, Paula. I'm a horny guy, but strictly straight."

"Okay."

"So he says, what about conjugal visits? And I say Father, my wife and I are divorced. And he says, not in the eyes of the church. And I'm thinking, sure, we got divorced, but that was to save your assets."

"Rigby—"

"So I looked into the rules, and I'm entitled. I was thinking maybe next time you come up, I could reserve the trailer."

She shook her head and looked as though she couldn't believe he'd asked, which hurt. "We're not divorced on a technicality. We're divorced."

"Seriously? You believe that?"

"Yes."

"Huh." He was surprised at how much the simple declaration on her part pained him.

"So how terrible is it in here?"

He shrugged. "It paid off, pleading out."

"Don't think I don't appreciate it. And the others. You saved us."

"Fuck the others, I did it for you and the kids. Don't think I wouldn't have loved to see Jerry Haskill in my place."

"Okay. I appreciate what you did."

"Anyway, minimum security's pretty soft. Got TV and a good gym. The priest I was talking about, he's taken an interest in me. I confessed to some shit once I'd been in for a little while, some things I'd been keeping from Father Daugherty."

"Huh."

She didn't ask what things they were, and he didn't push it.

"Are you seeing anyone?" he asked.

"Not really," she said.

"What's that mean?"

"Means not seriously."

"What's that mean?"

"We're not married anymore and you don't get to know everything."

He nodded. He wanted to keep asking, but he knew he wouldn't get another word out if she didn't want to talk. It really wasn't his business anymore anyway, was it? But that was crazy. "So I googled Kushik the other day."

She raised an eyebrow and looked around the room to make sure no one was listening.

"It's nothing. Just I came up with an article from the St. Louis paper about the school getting the painting. Jerry made a speech at the ceremony about his dear old uncle Glenn and his devotion to the school."

Paula shook her head. "Yeah, he's made it his mission to immortalize his legacy. I think he's convinced himself he didn't do it."

For just a second Rigby regretted it, taking the rap for that squirrelly bastard Haskill, who sat free and rich in St. Louis, but the thought that he'd done it for Paula and the kids landed him back in the world.

TEN MINUTES LATER, SHE was gone, and five minutes after that, he was in the library looking up a precedent for a fellow con, a half-literate country boy from San Berdoo County who'd gotten himself mixed up in a Ponzi scheme. It had been a long time since he'd consulted any law books, but he was getting the hang of it again and he had a feeling he could help get the kid off.

An hour after that, on the way back to his cell, he reflected on what he'd done. He'd never see Nina again, or Will Seghers, but he was proud of what they'd pulled off, and almost as much as he wished he could spend that money, he wished they could sit down over a drink and celebrate. Hell, he was even happy for young Keith getting a nest egg, despite his having had the gall to top his wife. In his cell now, he got to thinking about Paula and wondering why he'd ever thought he needed more than her. The more he thought about it, the less sense it made, but eventually, he supposed, he'd work it out.